They were lost. People kept shooting at them. Someone wanted her dead.

Mary worked really hard at *not* having a full-blown panic attack.

"It's dark," Gideon said flatly. "If we keep driving around, we're going to run out of gas before we find our way out of here. Let's wait for morning. Hole up."

Hole up? Was this actually her life, or one big, freaky nightmare? This morning, she'd just been Marysia O'Hurley, reclusive widow. Tonight, she was the target of multiple killers for reasons she didn't understand, and on the run with a sexy federal agent who was scaring the pants off her. And that was almost literal.

She'd been shot at three separate times, she couldn't go home, and she had the audacity to think *"sex"* every time she looked at Gideon Brand.

She was stuck in a car. In the middle of nowhere. Till morning. With six feet of big, bad, sexy male.

Some women would label that last bit lucky. Mary found it terrifying.

Dear Reader,

Marysia O'Hurley started out as the best friend of one of the main characters in my first HAVEN book, *Secrets Rising*, and she was so much fun, I couldn't resist creating a story just for her. In *Secrets Rising*, she played at being a psychic and discovered that Haven's earthquake had turned her power from pretend to real. In *Protected in His Arms*, follow Marysia as she deals with the dark side of her unexpected power and is forced to find the good in it when a U.S. Marshal needs her special skills. And soon, Marysia realizes it's not only the hot, sexy federal lawman who needs her to help him find a missing little girl—Marysia needs him because the kidnapper is after her, too.

Welcome back to Haven, West Virginia!

Love,

Suzanne McMinn

SUZANNE McMINN

Protected in His Arms

Silhouette®
Romantic
SUSPENSE

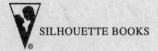 SILHOUETTE BOOKS

Recycling programs
for this product may
not exist in your area.

ISBN-13: 978-0-373-27612-7
ISBN-10:   0-373-27612-5

PROTECTED IN HIS ARMS

Copyright © 2008 by Suzanne McMinn

SUZANNE McMINN

Suzanne McMinn is an award-winning author of two dozen novels, including contemporary paranormal romance, romantic suspense and contemporary romantic comedy as well as a medieval trilogy. She lives on a farm in the mountains of West Virginia, where she is plotting her next book and enjoying the simple life with her family, friends and many, many cats. Check out her upcoming books and blog at www.suzannemcminn.com.

Chapter 1

Step down from the bench in seventy-two hours or the little girl dies.

U.S. Marshal Gideon Brand ran his hands over the rough stubble of his face. It had already been twelve hours since a federal judge's six-year-old granddaughter had been discovered missing. She'd disappeared on Gideon's watch.

The threatening message had arrived in the judge's inbox an hour later, time stamped 7:21 a.m. Eastern Standard, and all the forces of federal law enforcement were hard at work attempting to unscramble its path. They would fail. The nascent technology of the heavily encrypted e-mail bypassed central servers and would automatically erase itself in a matter of hours—destroying along with it all evidence of its origin. It was as close to foolproof as had ever been seen.

"You're supposed to be out of here already."

Gideon pivoted in his seat to find the head of the West Virginia judicial security division watching him with expressionless eyes honed from his military special ops background. A look that caused Gideon to believe, far too often, that he was *still* in special ops.

"Go home," Darren Tucker said. "Some rest will do you a world of good."

"I'm not tired."

"This isn't your case anymore. I know that's hard to accept, but that's the way it is."

Tucker was now assuming direct supervision of the operation.

Gideon was tempted to tell him where he could stick his case, and his pseudosympathy. Molly was more than a case. She was a human being and he had come to care for her more than he'd ever expected. Maybe she reminded him too much of what he'd lost, but this wasn't about him. It was about Molly.

Unleashing his anger on Tucker for his insensitivity and authoritarianism would do nothing to save her life. But the statement Judge Alcee Reinhold was in the process of preparing likely wouldn't save her either. Kidnappers rarely returned their victims, and the judge had a recent history of deadly intimidations against him that was believed to include the bombing of a small plane and the death of a federal agent.

"Go home," Tucker repeated.

"Seventy-two hours," Gideon said harshly as he stood. His chest hurt and his hands fisted at his sides.

Go home? Do nothing?

On any given day, he was responsible for investigating, analyzing and assessing threats and other inappropriate communications to sitting judges, as well as supervising protective detail, round the clock if necessary. He had a record of apprehensions and successful cases longer than his arm and he was being dismissed like a child who needed a nap.

Did they actually think he could just go home and suck his thumb while Molly's life hung in the balance?

"And there are only sixty of them left," Gideon added pointedly.

Darren Tucker knew when to keep his mouth shut. There were no platitudes to ease the awful fact that a man who may have killed a planeload of thirty-four innocent people in one fell swoop wouldn't hesitate to slaughter one more.

"We're doing everything we can," Gideon said, speaking the platitude for the commander. He heard the emotion he'd sworn to control come out in his voice. "Except not."

Bitterness stung deeply. He didn't agree with the

media blackout on information regarding Molly's kidnapping.

"Go home and go to bed," Tucker said flatly. "You have five minutes, then I'll have you escorted from the building."

The commander left the room. Tough love, that's what he'd said to Gideon when he told him he was dismissed from the case. More than dismissed from the case. Sent on forced leave. He'd taken the case too personally, become too emotionally involved. According to Tucker, this made him a danger to himself, other agents, even to Molly. He didn't agree, but he didn't get to choose.

Gideon left the building with nothing. The truth was he had no personal belongings at the office.

And the same was true of his apartment, he thought wryly as he parked his car and got out. His apartment was cold, with an overhanging sense of emptiness despite being marginally furnished. He looked at a photo of a smiling, bubble-blowing five-year-old Lizzie on the mantel over the fireplace where he'd never burned a log. Frozen in time, weeks before his daughter had died. Innocent, her life shining ahead of her, then gone in a blink.

Six months later, his marriage had fallen in line as if her murderer's second victim.

He pushed away the feelings that photo always inspired, the guilt and loss so deep, they couldn't be borne, and focused on the reason he kept it there, to remind himself of his purpose in life. Without that purpose, he'd have given up long ago.

Even with it, he swirled the sink drain a lot of days. He hadn't been able to save Lizzie. He hadn't even had a chance.

But Molly…

He had a chance to save her. It wasn't too late. Not yet. And there was no way he was walking away.

No one knew for sure why someone wanted Judge Alcee Reinhold off the bench. It could be revenge for a case on which the judge had already ruled or preparation for a case yet to come before the court. A case someone didn't want to have come before Judge Reinhold. Specifically, it was possible the intimidation against the judge was related to the Pittsburgh mafia infiltration of West Virginia and attempts to nail the ringleaders. The judge dealt with search warrants, wiretaps, secret grand jury testimony. Bribery for tip-offs was mafia stock in trade.

If the judge wasn't cooperating, they'd want him replaced. It was Gideon's current working theory, though no direct link between the attacks and the mafia had been made.

Stacks of files staggered in piles on the kitchen table. None of the materials were classified. They were mostly notes in his own hand, ideas, questions, scraps of random ideas and newspaper clippings about the Pittsburgh mafia.

He got a glass of water from the kitchen, sat down at the table and stared at the folders. He made himself feel nothing as he pored over his notes and every article, again. He could let emotion drive him, but he couldn't let it stand in his way.

The pile on the bottom contained clippings and notes from the plane explosion. It had been a dramatically deadly act. Suspicion from the beginning had centered on threats to Alcee Reinhold, who hadn't made the flight. Unfortunately, Robbie Buchanan, the federal agent assigned to escort him, had already been on board. If the bombing had indeed been intended for the judge, the Marshals couldn't prove it. They only knew how the perpetrator had gotten access to the plane to plant the bomb. The perpetrator had most likely masqueraded as a member of the construction staff and gotten through using a stolen ID. The bomb had been planted in the twin-propeller passenger plane's cargo hold.

But the investigation into the explosion had long ago grown cold, as had any clues to the identity of its mastermind. Agents had pored over security tapes, looking for the face of a killer, attempting to identify each person.

Gideon sat in the growing dusk of his apartment staring at the pile of clippings related to the attack on Flight 498. He read through them, one by one, for the four-thousandth time.

There was nothing new.

Except his level of desperation. Something wasn't right. He just didn't know what it was.

He grabbed the phone off an end table in the small living room and phoned Tucker.

"Brand here. I want to know what came out in that interview with the psychic," he clipped out. Impatient? Hell, yeah.

"What?"

"That psychic from Haven who called the airport, said Flight 498 was going to explode. There was a tracking ID for an interview outcome report, but I never received the file."

"Get some sleep, Brand."

"Did anyone actually talk to Marysia O'Hurley?"

"Yes, we talked to her. Dammit, Brand. Do you not see—"

"What was the outcome?"

"—you are obsessed! And you aren't thinking clearly!"

"What was the outcome?"

"She was an hysterical wife! Get a grip. Her husband was taking that flight. She admitted she was afraid of flying herself. Do you know how many crank calls they get at the airport every day? She's a whack job, and she didn't have anything to do with the bombing. She was thoroughly checked out. Get some sleep!"

The grainy photo in the newspaper clipping showed a slender, dark-haired woman with grieving eyes. She looked lost, even in the crowd of mourners photographed that day at the airport. Her eyes hit the camera dead-on, and there was nothing hysterical about them, even in the midst of shock.

"You remember what they said about Haven after that quake," Gideon said, and even as he spoke the words, he felt foolish. The tiny town of Haven, West Virginia, had been hit by an earthquake the year before and the aftermath had included a cable media circus of claims about "positive ions" triggering paranormal activity.

Earthquakes were uncommon in West Virginia, but the event itself wasn't all that had been strange about the four-point-three shock. The news had been full of panicked homeowners reporting bursts of horizontal light and a reddish haze in the air. Fire trucks had responded to a variety of locations, but had found no flames to douse. One resident had called in a paranormal detective after a young boy was found, scratched and confused, along a roadside claiming to have been trapped inside a red ball of light.

A spokesperson from the Paranormal Activity Institute had called the quake, in combination with existing atmospheric conditions of low pressure and dense moisture at the time, the "perfect storm," labeling the bursts of reddish light "foundational movement" for oncoming supernatural incidents.

Anything can happen in Haven now, the PAI spokesperson had stated.

It had been quite an eye-rolling interview, and it had played over and over in news reports. Even Gideon hadn't missed it, despite the small amount of television he watched. The furor of the story had eventually died down, and if anything genuinely paranormal had ever happened in Haven, Gideon didn't know about it. He certainly hadn't taken any of it seriously.

Following the kidnapping, he'd returned to head-quarters and requested the files on all the interview outcomes going back to the plane bombing. He'd gotten every file, immediately, except the one on Marysia O'Hurley, the supposed psychic from Haven.

This evening, he'd made a specific request for her file alone.

Twenty minutes later, he'd been suspended.

"Do you hear yourself talking, Brand?" Tucker asked simply.

"Yeah. I do." Gideon was silent for a heavy beat. The something-wasn't-right feeling in his gut itched at him.

He heard a very subtle click on the line. Suspended and…wiretapped?

His pulse went dead still.

Slowly, he held the phone away from his ear. He could hear Tucker, distantly now, asking him if he'd lost his mind. He used his pocketknife to quickly take apart the bottom of the receiver and found the tiny listening device nestled inside.

Putting the phone back to his ear, he snapped, "Did you wire my phone?"

"What the hell are you talking about now? Of course we didn't wire your phone."

Gideon punched the Off button.

Either the commander was lying—in which case, he was done talking to him—or someone else had wired his phone.

A perpetrator who was an expert at bombs and security infiltration and high-tech communication.

As he raced out of the apartment, Gideon wondered why it had never occurred to him before that the same perpetrator who could be behind both a bombing and a kidnapping could be one of his own.

Gideon was in and out of the southern district office in under seven minutes, breaking all the rules, bypassing all security except at the gate. Security was sometimes not much more than a facade when you knew your way around. It was late, and the guard at the post didn't realize Brand had been put on leave. Maybe he didn't get the memo.

The door to his office was closed and locked, though the lock had not been changed. He powered on the desktop unit, found he still had access to the databank on the network.

He typed in Marysia O'Hurley's name, did a search. There was nothing there. No interview outcome report file tracking ID. An ID had been in the system mere hours earlier. He'd used the number to request the file from the secure records room.

The computer screen went sharply black, then a white screen with black letters appeared: *You are attempting to access an unapproved area.*

The hair prickled at the nape of his neck. Network usage was tracked and his access had just been cut off from somewhere inside the building.

He scraped back his chair, headed for the empty, night-lit hallway. Someone opened fire and he heard the audible rush of a bullet past his ear. Blood pounded in his veins as he evaded and struck back. He fired in the direction of the blast in the same second he leaped for the door to the stairs, took them in flying bounds to the underground parking.

The guard at the gate reached for the phone inside his booth.

Reaching the gate, he had his window down and his gun out, and before the guard could speak or attempt to draw, Gideon pointed his GLOCK.

"Open the gate."

He was through.

For the first time since he'd heard that shot, he felt his hands shake, reaction kicking in. No internal alarm had gone off in the building. He'd been shot at *inside* headquarters. He forcibly shut down the part of his brain that registered emotion, firmed his grip on the wheel as he steadied his pulse, his Impala speeding through the maze of dark streets. He braked at a light long enough to see that the cross-street was deserted, then zoomed through it and up the interstate on-ramp.

He'd gotten away clean, but there was no going home. And he had a real bad feeling whoever had shot at him inside the building had no need to follow him. All he could do now was hope he got there first—and alive. By pulling that gun on the guard, he had just become a wanted man.

Armed and dangerous. His fellow Marshals would be ordered to shoot to kill. His life had just taken on the value of dirt.

Molly's life was on the line. His own was only important in that context. As was, now, Marysia O'Hurley's.

When he flicked the headlamps on as he sped up I-79 North, the sign whizzing by read, Haven, 22 miles.

Chapter 2

Somebody was going to get into that Impala tonight and have sex. And that somebody was her.

For one wild, panicky breath, Marysia O'Hurley wanted the fever dream of delicious lust that hit her with the flash of perception to be real. *Hot ripples scorching her skin. His fingers teasing inside her. Her muscles clenching around him. Her voice, sobbing at the shock wave of pure pleasure…*

No, no, no. She blocked the sensory images assaulting her so hard that her knees nearly collapsed under her.

The man getting out of said Impala that had pulled into the parking lot next to her car was tall, built, effortlessly sexy. She'd just bet he was as good with his hands as she imagined. It was all she could do to not stare at his ropey-sinewy body and go right back to fantasyland.

And it *was* fantasy. Not any projection of soon-to-be reality.

First off, she was hardly Miss America, and despite the see-all way his gaze pinned her, she didn't have a history of come-ons by rugged, sexy, impossibly erotic strangers in parking lots as if she was living out some kind of *True Confessions* story line.

Second, she was crazy, certifiable, wasn't she? The cacophony of uncomfortable intuitive flashes that had taken over her life made her feel like a satellite picking up too many signals—most of which were likely products of her ridiculous imagination.

Maybe somebody *was* going to get lucky in that Impala tonight. But it wasn't going to be her.

She hadn't gotten lucky in a long time.

Not that she cared.

Marysia averted her gaze from the man now standing by the Impala. She felt the man grab her arm.

"Are you all right?"

No. Not really.

Not at all.

She refused to meet his eyes, stared down at the lean chest of the so-sexy stranger. Even his voice was sexy. Wow, he'd moved fast. Not that the parking lot was huge. Haven's one tiny grocery store had just a row of parking in the front and another row along one side. And that this was the biggest store in town said a lot about Haven, West Virginia. It served as everything from grocery store to hardware and feed store to fast-food deli, not to mention game checking station, movie rental and community gossip hub.

"I said, are you all right?" he repeated.

"I'm fine. Thank you. Excuse me."

An older lady and a boy came around the corner of the store, heading toward their car, packages in hand.

He let go of her arm and she ran, actually ran, around the side of the building and into the grocery store. Her heart hammered like mad.

She needed cinnamon. Not sex. Cinnamon.

Baking. She loved to bake. Baking was normal.

She just wanted things to go back to normal.

Normal was a town in Illinois. At least that was part of the pep talk she'd been trying on herself lately. There was no such thing as normal. Not for anyone, much less for her, and if she stopped telling herself that normal was something she needed, then she'd be able to relax. Deal with things. Accept life as it was. Crazy was the new black.

She was half Polish, half Italian, and she'd been married to an Irish guy. What did people expect from her anyway?

It was nearly closing time. She raced through the store, grabbed a small jar of ground cinnamon, some flour, then a bag of apples, and headed for the checkout. No. She needed ice cream. She definitely needed ice cream. She picked out a gallon of vanilla bean from the freezer case, juggling it with the other things until she got up front.

"Looks like somebody's makin' something good tonight," the Foodway checker said as she rang up the items. "Yum. Wish I was going to your house."

Mary tugged a ten out of her wallet.

"Pie," she said.

There was nothing more normal than apple pie and vanilla ice cream. She handed the bill to the girl behind the register. She looked like she was about nineteen. Mary hadn't seen her before, so Keely must have just hired her.

She could see her friend coming up the aisle from the back of the store. Keely had spotted her.

The girl made change. She dropped the coins in Mary's hand. The all-too-familiar-now snap of what sometimes felt like electricity jolted her. Mary met the girl's eyes, the coins hot in her fist now.

She was a pretty girl with big, trust-me eyes, and she was going to get fired tomorrow for stealing.

"Hey," Keely Schiffer said, reaching the check-out. "I thought that was you I saw whizzing through the store like somebody shot you out of a cannon. Not planning to stop and say hey to your best friend tonight?"

"I was in a hurry. And you looked busy in your office, so I didn't want to bother you."

"Was that two excuses for the price of one?"

Mary didn't argue the point her friend drove home all too well. Yeah, so she was a little antisocial and a lot in denial.

She looked away from her friend's piercing eyes, her gaze landing on the stack of weekly newspapers sitting next to the register. She focused on the headlines as if she was interested. Construction was starting on a new field house at the high school. The mayor was up for reelection. A mobile home fire was under investigation. The deer population was on the rise.

"I was thinking we should get together, go shopping or something," Keely said. "I hardly see you—"

"I can't," Mary said. She gathered her packages. "I'm sorry."

She thought about telling her the new checker was a thief, but then Keely was going to find out on her own pretty soon if that were true, wasn't she? Just like the librarian was going to find out she was pregnant next week, and somebody was going to get in that Impala in the parking lot and have some superfabulous sex tonight.

Or Mary was just crazy like everybody said. Either way, keeping her lip zipped seemed like a good choice. Even if Keely was maybe the only person in Haven who might, just might, not call her crazy. But Mary knew Keely herself had kept her own experiences after the earthquake close to the vest, even if she had shared one of those experiences with Mary.

Or maybe it was Mary who didn't want to talk about it and she was projecting, wrongly. A piano teacher by trade, she'd spent ten years hobbying as pretend psychic at community fairs and school carnivals. Until the earthquake had changed everything. The real thing wasn't quite as much fun.

And what was the point because nobody believed her? People thought she was crazy, other than the occasional crackpot who, thanks to the media circus surrounding her husband's death, called her for the "psychic" services she no longer offered.

She gave Keely a quick hug. "I'm sorry. I gotta go. I'll call you later."

"No, you won't!" Keely called after her.

No, she probably wouldn't.

The man was still there, now leaning against the Impala and watching her.

She walked between their cars to her driver's-side door, juggling packages along with her oversized purse.

"I'm sorry about your husband."

She dropped the bag of apples.

"What?" She stared at him over the top of his car. It had been nine months since Danny had died. She was used to sympathetic platitudes, even from strangers. But how this stranger knew who she was... She'd never seen him before, she was certain of that.

"I know how it feels to lose someone. I know you know how it feels, too."

"How did you—" She broke off, stared at him

again. A floodlight on the building revealed his features. Square jaw, intensely jade eyes, planed cheeks, a full, straight lean mouth. Dark, thick, almost military-short hair.

How could she forget him if she'd met him before today?

He was the epitome of hot, his mile-long legs clad in worn blue jeans and a plain white T-shirt, untucked yet stretching over impressive pecs, revealing forearms tightly muscled. His pose was lazy like a coiled cat. He wore the bearing of a man who did nothing while he looked as if he could do anything.

Leap tall buildings in single bounds, for example. Action hero material. Definitely.

He belonged on a movie poster with curling flames as his backdrop.

Any woman who got into that Impala with him would be a very lucky woman, indeed.

She felt jittery, sweaty.

It took everything in her to block the sensory assault again. Could she be more lame? Fantasizing about sex with a stranger in a parking lot. Stranger danger, that's what he was.

And he certainly looked dangerous. Intelligent, street-tough, almost ridiculously gorgeous—but gorgeous like a long, sharp knife. Nope, she didn't need any of that.

She struggled to get her breathing and her nerves under control.

"How do you know me?" she asked, repeating the question she'd only half managed to get out before.

"I lost a friend on Flight 498."

Could they have crossed paths at the airport that day? She'd gone there, too, just as had all the other passengers' family members. They'd stood around, waiting for official information as if some miracle was going to be announced.

She'd known everyone. In her mind.

Lots of people were scared of flying, especially smaller planes. But just because she'd had a severe and highly imaginative panic attack the day her husband had gotten on one, and just because his plane had ended up actually blowing up, didn't mean she was a real psychic. It just meant she was an hysterical wife.

Coincidence. Nothing more.

It was safer to think that way.

She'd been scared to read anything about the crash victims later. Crazy, that's what she was. No need to confirm it. And if the victims *had* matched up to those whose lives had flashed before her eyes that day… She didn't want to know that either.

She tried to speak to the stranger, to tell him she was sorry for his loss, to speak those empty platitudes of sympathy she knew so well. But her throat felt too tight because suddenly he was right there, in front of her.

He picked up the bag of apples, held them toward her. She stared at him. She didn't want to take the apples from him. She didn't want to touch his hand as he handed them to her. Hot instinct ripped through her, even stronger than her so-called psychic flashes. This was women's instinct.

She just wanted to get out of there. Why did the parking lot feel so empty suddenly?

There was no one else outside the store. The air carried the scent of a coming storm. Wind rustled in the trees behind the building. The occasional car moved down the two-lane highway that led to the re-stored town square with its beautiful courthouse, cobbled sidewalks and quaint shops and restaurants. Haven, West Virginia, one letter short of Heaven, the cheerful welcome sign coming into town boasted. Surrounded by thick woods of oak, maple and walnut, and the sloped pastures and Gothic-style farmhouses of the Appalachian Mountains, the simple, sleepy scenery backed up the town's claim.

The pace was no different. Simple. Sleepy. It was a typical early summer night. Time for businesses to put up Closed signs, kids to be tucked into bed, Mary to go home to another lonely evening.

Action-movie-poster man didn't belong here.

"How do you know me?" she repeated warily.

"I went to your house, but you were leaving. I followed you here. We need to talk."

Her throat completely closed up.

Screw the apples. Get in the car, drive away. Her pulse thumped and she had trouble thinking.

Was he stalking her? What if he followed her

home? Wild possibilities tumbled through her mind. Maybe she was being hysterical.

Maybe she should go back in the store, get Keely. Keely could call the police and—

"I need your help," he continued. "And you don't know it, but you need mine. We don't have much time."

What?

"I can't help you." And the only way he could help *her* was to go away.

"I think you can. And I think you're in danger."

Yes, yes, so did she. From him. He was gorgeous, but a lunatic.

Very, very sad for the women of the world.

She had to get around him to get back to the store. How was she going to do that? Her mind ran jagged, panicky laps, trying to figure out the best way out of the spot she was in.

"I forgot something I meant to get. I have to go back into the store."

"No."

No? Her heart jumped with both feet into her throat when he set the apples down on the top of her car.

Relief socked her hard when another car pulled into the parking lot.

She was saved. Thank God.

The dark car screeched to a stop and a window rolled down. Bullets sprayed as the world rocked into slow motion and she screamed.

Chapter 3

Horror gripped Marysia but there was no time for that. The stranger pushed her, and her knees hit the asphalt as she slammed to the ground, her shopping bag flying. Panic roared through her veins and she could barely think, just crawl, desperately.

Run! She wanted to run. More gunshots cracked over her head and her heart boomed in her ears.

She heard tires screeching and a distant shout from the direction of the front of the store, the jangle of the store's bell over the door. She whipped her head around, saw the dark car gone as quickly as it had come, scrambled up from her hands and knees.

Run! But before she could, he was there, the

stranger, ripping open the door of his Impala, pushing her inside as from the corner of her eye she saw the dark car screeching back.

It hadn't gone away. It had merely turned around in the parking lot, was coming back for more.

Diving, she took cover inside the car as more shots blasted the air. She heard a crash, then nothing. Desperate breaths clawed her lungs. Before she could do anything, breathe, think, move, the stranger was inside, shoving her over to the driver's seat.

He had a gun. Oh, God.

He had a gun!

"Drive," he grated.

She blinked, panic and shock drumming wildly inside her. She saw the attacker's car in the rearview, crashed into a building at the side of the parking lot where Keely kept propane and tanks for sale.

"Drive!" He shouted this time. His hot jade eyes seared her. "Get out of here before he gets out of that car and comes back!"

"The store— My friend—"

"He doesn't want your friend. He wants you."

His words registered, but she couldn't process them. Why would anyone want to kill *her?*

And yet… Those bullets had been nothing if not incredibly real.

The Impala sprang to life as she turned the key, tires screaming backward. The shoulder strap of her purse tangled across her chest, the bag heavy in her lap, wedging between her body and the wheel. She saw Keely and the checkout girl run back into the store, saw the attacker's car door push open, a shadow escape, then the world behind her turned bright orange. The Impala hit the highway and she floored the gas, raw horror tearing through her.

Hardly in control of the car, she swerved to miss an oncoming vehicle. The car spun on gravel at the shoulder, and she braked to a skidding stop.

Breath backed up, harsh and cold, in her lungs.

Huge billows of black smoke filled the air behind them. Flames—

"We've got to go back! It exploded!" What exploded, she wasn't sure—the attacker's car, the propane. The store! Oh, God, the store. "We've got to make sure everyone is okay!"

Keely was back there! A killer was back there, too. But he was gone, he'd run away….

And there was a crazy stranger right here in the car with her.

A crazy stranger with a gun.

He'd protected her back there, though. Protected her from the attacker, protected her by forcing her to drive the car away from the blast.

"They went back in the store. They're fine. And we're not. Not yet. I need to talk to you. I'll explain everything. But not here! Drive!"

Her head reeled. He was, she realized, pointing the gun at her.

"Don't hurt me," she breathed harshly.

"I'm not going to hurt you. I'm trying to save your life. Dammit, drive!"

She hit the gas. The car slammed forward, back on the road. They were driving with no lights. She didn't know where the lights were. She fumbled madly for a switch, not finding it, following the road in the lights from roadside buildings, from memory.

Stay calm. He just wanted to talk, that had to be it. He wanted to talk. He was crazy, maybe, and he wanted to talk. She'd talk to him, then he'd let her go. Or kill her.

But she couldn't let herself think that way. She had to think of ways to escape. She'd drive to the police station.

She was in control of the car, wasn't she? Except for that gun thing.

"Turn there."

She didn't want to turn there. That was a back road. A country back road twisting out into the boonies. He wanted to explain. Fine, she'd love an explanation. But she wanted to talk somewhere safe, like the police station.

He grabbed the wheel when she didn't slow down and they careened while she nearly had a heart attack, grappling for control, hitting the brake, barely missing a guardrail as they swerved over a bridge that spanned the river.

Dark woods whizzed past as she regained control

of the car. There was no regaining control of her wildly pounding pulse.

She was getting out of this car!

She screeched to a stop, tried to grab open the door. His grip held her fast. She slapped at him with her other hand, not caring, let him shoot her. God, what would he do if she didn't get out of this car?

He had her with both arms, both of them half falling out of the open door of the car, him on top of her. Her harsh breaths seared her lungs and his fiery eyes slammed her.

"I'm not going to drive anywhere else! I'm not going anywhere with you!" she spat out breathlessly. She was going to die anyway.

Was that fear or one of her nutso psychic flashes? She didn't know anymore. She struggled again and must have caught him in a weak moment because she managed to kick at him sideways, scrambling to her feet as she pushed out the door.

She was off and running.

For about two seconds and he was on top of her and she was down, the asphalt biting into her knees again, tearing through her denim capris, then she slammed face down. She barely registered the physical pain.

"Just let me go. Please. Let me go home." She was begging and she didn't care. "Please don't hurt me."

Rape her. He was going to rape her. *That* was the deal about sex and his Impala! She'd just misread her impressions, probably because she was sex-starved.

Oh, God. This was no pleasure fantasy. Panic flooded her.

"Stop it!" he demanded roughly, holding her down, her arms pinned, his hard body making her attempts to kick backward at him useless. Exhausted, sobbing, she realized she was out of control, so far out of control.

She tried to get her breathing in order, tried to think. She had to use her brain. That was the only hope she had.

"I'm not going to hurt you."

He'd said that before. She didn't believe him. She couldn't see more than a half view of him from her position, cheek down on the hard road.

"Yes, you are!" she cried wildly. "You kidnapped me. You held a gun to me. You're pinning me down. You forced me down this deserted road. You're hurting me right now!"

"I'm trying to save your life! Listen to me!"

Out of control. She was still out of control.

She swallowed hard. Stop panicking! The order to herself was all but useless, but she faked it.

Calm.

Act calm. "Okay. I'm listening."

Use your brain, she reminded herself. Find out what he wanted. She tried to breathe, in, out, calm. Not calm at all. And her brain…

Fried.

"What— What was it you wanted to talk to me

about?" Her voice came out ragged, a sob choking her throat. He wanted to save her life? She hadn't needed any lifesaving until he'd shown up, him and whoever was after him.

There was no reason, no reason at all, anyone would be after *her*.

"There's a little girl. Six years old. She's missing."

It was the last thing she'd expected him to say, and she couldn't think straight.

"I'm sorry. You should call the police. They have people who do that, find missing children."

"They can't help me. You can. You knew about that plane bombing, didn't you?"

She went dead still. Stunned. Again.

He suddenly moved off her, twisted her around, pulling her up to face him. He held her shoulders with both hands. He wasn't letting go of her and she was scared to try to run again. She shook like a leaf.

The night closed in dark around them, seeming to swirl with shadows. Thunder banged. She felt sick, afraid of dying, and he—

He looked fearsomely in control. Action hero on the set.

"No. No, I didn't."

"Yes, you did. Maybe you know more than you think you know. Maybe someone else thinks so, too."

Pain, palpable pain, seemed to radiate off him in waves, wrap around her, and she struggled to push it back from suffocating her.

She was in pain. *She* was in danger—from him. She didn't know anything about any little girl.

She couldn't just *decide* to know something. The things she knew, they hit her, like wild shots in the dark. Images, impressions, sometimes smells and sounds. Truths and lies. It was nothing she could control. Nothing she *wanted* to control.

And she was wrong, mostly wrong, she was sure of it, and even if she was right, it was too little, too late. And she couldn't handle her own pain much less anyone else's.

Maybe you know more than you think you know. Maybe someone else thinks so, too.

What was he saying? That the attack at the store had been someone after her? Because she knew something? And what did that have to do with a missing girl? The plane bombing had been nine months ago.

"I can't help you. I'm sorry. Please let me go!"

"I can't do that," he persisted. "And trust me, you don't want me to. That shooting back at the store? That was about you."

No, no, no. That wasn't possible. Until he spoke, she didn't realize she'd said those words out loud.

"It is very possible. In fact," he went on grimly, "it's probable."

"Why?"

"There is a little girl who is going to die in less than three days if we don't find her. And there is a very good chance the person holding her is the same man who killed your husband and thirty-three other people on Flight 498."

Information overload. She couldn't put it all together.

His eyes on her were bright, sharp, searing her in the thick night. She suddenly felt almost disembodied. None of this could be happening. None of this made sense.

What could that bombing have to do with a little girl's kidnapping?

"I don't understand."

"You can't go home. If you go home, you're going to die."

"That's crazy!"

"Yes," he said quite seriously. "It *is* crazy."

The increasing humidity of the night seemed to close in on her, suffocating her. Crazy. The whole world had gone crazy.

"Are you— Are you some kind of police or something?" she demanded.

Suddenly the deadly capable way he had of handling himself, handling gunfire, hit her. She'd have been killed back there if not for his quick actions and reactions. He'd gotten her out of the way before the explosion, too. He was like a well-trained machine.

But he'd also held a gun to her head and forced her down this lonely road, nearly killing them both. He claimed that was to save her life, too.

"Who are you?" she repeated thinly when he didn't respond.

"My name is Gideon Brand. Until a few hours ago, I was a U.S. Marshal investigating threats to a federal judge that we believe started with that plane bombing. The latest threat came to life with the kidnapping of that judge's granddaughter. A six-year-old girl I was sworn to protect. I failed her. I won't rest until I find her, and I'm going to find her alive if I have to move heaven and earth to do it. And right now, that means moving you, whether you like it or not, whether you believe me or not. Whoever blew up that plane and kidnapped Molly thinks you know something.

"They want you dead now," he went on. "I want to know why. And they want me dead now, too, because I asked the wrong questions. Questions about you."

She swallowed hard.

"I don't know anything about a little girl! I don't know anything about the bombing!" She didn't. Truly, she didn't.

"Someone thinks you do. Something you said when you were interviewed after the bombing made someone think you do. But as long as nobody took you seriously, that was fine."

She could barely even remember the interview after the bombing. Officials had talked to her, yes. They'd blown off her initial call to the airport, to the police, and hadn't taken her seriously afterward either. She was glad. She'd been in shock and the craziness of her sensory projections hadn't done anything to help. They hadn't saved Danny anyway, so what good were they?

That someone actually thought she knew something, something that could point to a killer—

Terror wrapped her tight and she had the intense urge to run right into those woods behind her and never stop. But the wilds around Haven were home to bears and wolves, not just pretty deer. And tonight, maybe a murderous madman, too.

The madman who'd run out of that car in Haven right before it exploded. They hadn't driven that far away.

Her nerves felt like they were going to blow up. What had happened to apple pie and ice cream? Another quiet evening in almost Heaven?

"Nobody should take me seriously!" she raged at the stranger, anger suddenly boiling up inside her. "I'm a fake! I'm hysterical! I'm crazy! Haven't you heard? I am not a psychic!"

She pushed to her feet and he let her go. She saw her purse, lying in a heap on the road where it had slung off her shoulder in her escape from the car. She reached down, picked it up, scooping back into it the items that had fallen out—the cell phone that only got a signal when she was in the city, the flavored lip gloss that was just about all she ever wore for makeup, a pen from the bank. Her mother had given her mace a couple of years ago. Why, oh why, had she decided when she'd cleaned out her overweight purse the last time that the mace was what had to go?

She backed a step at a time from the stranger.

He stood, and even from several feet away, she felt as if he towered over her. Six feet of scary male. She was not a small woman, but she was no match for him. The woods behind her felt thick and ominous. The attacker was out there, somewhere.

Not that this stranger should be any less frightening to her and yet—

The world around her, the world gone mad, was scaring her even more than he was.

"I don't think you're crazy," he said.

"If you don't think I'm crazy, then you're the crazy one." Her voice broke. God, don't start crying. She willed herself not to let a tear fall. "I want to go home."

She wanted her little two-bedroom house wrapped with perennial gardens and just enough space from neighbors to feel secluded on its small acreage. Home.

She felt a sob filling her throat, but crying wasn't going to fix anything.

"You can't go home. You'll end up dead. And so will Molly."

And she heard it in his voice again, the pain. Whatever was or wasn't true here, that was real. He cared about this missing girl. His energy was strong and the signals bouncing off him now nearly knocked her down.

"Then I want to go to the police."

"You can't do that either. It's not safe."

Going to the *police* wasn't safe?

"How do I know anything you're saying is the truth? How do I even know you're a U.S. Marshal?"

He reached into his pocket, flashed open his credentials. She had to take a step toward him to see them in the last bit of light streaking through the dark clouds. There was an identification card with a badge that looked like a star within a circular ring.

Very Wild West-looking.

She lifted her gaze to his hard, deadly one, and shivered. Oh, God. That had really looked like an official badge, but she was scared to believe it. For all she knew, he'd bought it on the Internet. Or at a Western wear store.

"If you're a U.S. Marshal, then why were you taking me down this back road instead of to the authorities?"

The storm that had been coming hit and hit hard. Her clothes instantly soaked to her skin. Droplets of water rained down the stranger's face.

Gideon's face.

He had a name: Gideon Brand. His face shadowed hard and uncompromising in the wild night. Long, sharp knife, that's what he was. He was like a walking lean, mean, killing machine. And yet he said he was one of the good guys.

Her heart clanged in her chest, fear returning full force. He looked scarily intimidating, but his energy kept slamming her with the opposite impression, that he *was* one of the good guys. That he was telling her the truth.

And when he spoke, she'd never more in her life wished she could think someone was lying.

"Because," he said, "I have reason to believe the person who blew up that plane, the person who's holding Molly, the person who wants you and me dead tonight is also a U.S. Marshal."

Chapter 4

"I tried to get the record of your interview," Gideon told her. "Then I was put on forced leave and somebody tried to kill me. And now someone wants you dead, too. I don't think this sequence of events is a coincidence."

Marysia O'Hurley watched him with frightened, dilated eyes. Blue eyes. Startling blue that the black-and-white newspaper photograph hadn't done justice. Rain soaked her clothes to her slender body, revealing every fragile tremor and sway, but she'd already shown him she was strong. She was scared, too, and he wished to God he could take that horror out of her eyes, but it was there because she was starting to believe him.

He had to hold on to that tenuous faith or even now, she'd cut and run. He'd catch her again. He had no doubt of that, but in the process he might hurt her again. And for some reason he didn't want to hurt this woman.

"I need you to believe in me," he said, afraid to take a step toward her, still afraid she'd run. "And I need to believe in you. We need each other, or Molly's going to die." He couldn't let himself forget that this was all about Molly. "I don't think you're hysterical. I don't think you're crazy. I think you do know things and I think you're afraid it's true. I think it's true. And that is a huge leap of faith I'm taking here because I am believing the unbelievable, and I'm doing it for Molly because you're the only hope I've got. I need you to take that leap with me because I think I'm your only hope, too. If you go to the cops, if you go to the Marshals, you're going to end up dead."

She was shaking her head at him, wildly.

He took a chance, reached for her arm.

"Let's get back to the car," he shouted over the growing noise of the wind and rain. "We have to get out of here."

"I can't help you!"

Her voice came out low and broken, hardly audible over the storm.

He was close to her now. She hadn't bucked at his hold. Not yet, anyway. He could feel the trembling of her body through his grip on her arm.

"Yes, you can."

"I'm not a real psychic!" Her eyes blazed at him, vulnerable and bright. Broken. Something about her was so broken.

He didn't want to see that. He didn't want to know that. He didn't want to be touched by her.

"I think you are. I think you think so, too."

"No, I don't!"

He realized she was crying. That wasn't just rain streaking down her face, it was tears.

His heart, the one he didn't want to have anymore, ripped just a bit.

Molly. He had to focus on Molly. What emotion he had left inside him had to go to her. He had a job to do. The clock was ticking, and he had nothing to go on but what he had to hope and pray was in the mind of the woman in front of him.

"Get in the car!" he shouted over the wind. "Please," he added, softer, because she was still ripping at his heart or because he didn't want to scare her any more than she was already, he couldn't have said for sure. Or didn't want to say, even to himself.

If things were different, if he wasn't the shell of a man that he was, if she wasn't terrified out of her mind, if their situation wasn't so desperate, he might have noticed the perfect package that she was with her wild, dark hair, luminous skin and candy-sweet body.

But he *was* a shell of a man, she *was* terrified and their situation *was* desperate. And that made her nothing but part of the job.

She stood there staring at him, her hair plastered to her head, shivering, shaking, scared still, dammit, but there was no more time to waste. They had to get the hell out of here, and fast.

He tugged her arm, prodding her to move then run. He opened the passenger-side door and she slid inside. He got in, turned the key in the engine, flipped on the lights.

"I don't know what you think I can do," she said. "I don't know anything about any little girl. I can't tell you where she is, who's holding her. I can't just, snap, come up with information. It doesn't work like that."

He swung his gaze to her, let a tight beat pass. Was she admitting it did work, that she did have some kind of psychic ability? He let a second beat pass and it was one beat too many.

Lights strobed across the rearview mirror. A car had turned down the road.

Adrenaline surged, sharp. Run or deal.

He reached for the woman beside him, shoving her head into her knees, grabbed his GLOCK, slammed down the driver's-side button for the passenger window as the other car screeched to a stop. One second for recognition of the driver and his intent. Two to fire.

Jimmy Guarino's skull thunked hard against the headrest before he slumped forward over the wheel, the gun still in the mafia underling's hand.

Rain pounded.

He'd studied the face of every known mafioso in the Pittsburgh family. Organized crime involvement in the case was no longer a working theory. And within the space of hours, a federal agent and a mafia gun had tried to take him out.

He yanked the car into gear even as Marysia O'Hurley sat up, took one look out the window in the second before he hit the gas, saw blood and screamed. The Impala flew down the narrow road.

"You killed somebody!" she shouted.

"It was him or me," he said grimly, gaze locked on the road. "And you." They'd almost gotten killed, again. He didn't have time to sort it all out now. Or calm her down. "We have to get out of here."

The windshield wipers slapped against the glass. She was silent now. He shot a glance her way. She was silent and shaking.

The road was narrow, so narrow that if two cars were to pass, one would have to move off onto the shoulder—or what passed for a shoulder on this country road. The blacktop was rutted and, in places, the bank dropped off steeply. There was a creek somewhere below. The road rolled up and downhill, at times low enough to see the dark water streaming parallel to the lane. Typical West Virginia backcountry, complete with blind curves and other narrow roads shooting off, some paved, some not.

"Where are we going?" Fear threaded through her voice.

At least she'd stopped screaming.

Closed in the car with her, he could smell the scent of her herbal shampoo, hear the soft panting gasps of her breath, see the damp tangle of her hair around her neck.

"I don't know." For the first time, he thought about gas. He'd been in too much of a hurry to get to Haven—and then get out of Haven—for the status of the gauge to register until now.

Obviously, he hadn't been planning to go on the lam today. That was almost funny. Except not.

Jimmy Guarino didn't work alone.

"That's not making me feel better! I don't even know if you're really a U.S. Marshal! You just killed somebody!"

"He was a mafia hitman."

"He was *what?*"

That, apparently, had not been the right thing to tell her.

"I don't have time to explain now."

"Of course. You know what? Nobody was shooting at me before you came along! How do I know anything you say is true? Some little girl was kidnapped. Somebody's threatening a judge. Somebody in the U.S. Marshals is involved. Now it's the mafia!

Maybe you're just a lunatic and the cops are hunting you down! Maybe you took me as a hostage! Maybe you're a serial killer. Or a rapist!"

She was starting to sound hysterical and he couldn't blame her. People kept trying to kill her.

And she wasn't completely convinced he wasn't one of them.

"I'm not going to hurt you. That guy back there? He was trying to kill you. I'm trying to save your life."

"I don't know that!"

Trust. He needed her trust.

She'd had a few more minutes to think now and she was *re*thinking going with him. And as he slowed for a low-water bridge in a sharp turn, she grabbed the handle, opened the door.

He skidded to a stop, barely keeping the car from going over the concrete bridge into the creek raging with rainwater now, grabbed her before she could make good her escape.

"Let me go!" she screamed.

He had hold of her and he wasn't letting her get away, not this time. They had no time to waste.

"Dammit, stop it!" he ordered, her efforts futile but panicked and strong.

Always stronger than she looked, this Marysia O'Hurley.

"You have to trust me," he grated roughly, reached over her with his free hand to yank the car door shut again. His arm brushed her soft, round breasts. Her innocent herbal scent swirled his nostrils, stronger. For a second, he nearly stopped breathing. A twitch of sharp, hot awareness blindsided him.

He was suddenly, unbelievably, aroused, desire pumping along with adrenaline as she fought him. The only explanation he could come up with was that it had been a hell of a long time since he'd been laid.

Her eyes, wild, met his, and he slammed down on his ridiculous reaction to her. His needs had no place here, none at all. People were trying to kill them. Sex was not on the agenda.

"You won't even tell me where we're going!" she yelled at him.

"I don't know where we're going," he admitted. "Right now, tonight, in this minute, I'm just trying to keep us safe."

And sitting here on this low water bridge wasn't his definition of safe. Still holding her with one fist, gripping her hand too tightly but afraid to let go, he reached for his gun again.

Reached and, slowly, handed it to her. She dropped her gaze from him to the gun to him again. She didn't take it.

"What are you doing?" she gasped.

"Giving you my gun."

He could only pray he wasn't making the biggest mistake of his life. As long as she felt vulnerable— and God knew he understood why she did—she'd keep trying to run. He had to give her some sense of power, control. He had to earn her trust.

And hope she didn't use it to blow his head off.

"I need you to trust me," he said grimly. "We need to trust each other. Take it," he said when she still didn't pick it up.

He let go of her, giving himself the distance he desperately needed.

"Just don't run," he went on. "Take the gun. I don't want you to be scared of me. I'm not going to hurt you."

"I don't know much about guns," she said, almost blankly, as if she were in shock. And she probably *was* in shock.

"I'll teach you sometime. For now, just remember that it's loaded."

"So I can shoot you?"

"So you'll trust me, I hope."

He saw her throat move in the darkness illuminated only by the dim light of the dash and the headlights reflecting back at them where they struck the rushing water. He'd stopped the car pointed straight at the creek in the sharp curve. Tree branches swayed with the gusting wind.

"Aren't you afraid I'll shoot you?"

"Yes." He hit the gas, getting out of there.

He glanced her way. She gripped the forty-caliber GLOCK, lifting it a few inches, keeping it warily pointed downward.

"Kind of a dramatic gesture, don't you think?" she said, eyeing him carefully.

Suspicious still.

"Kind of a dramatic situation," he replied carefully.

"I don't like drama," she said. "I don't like danger. I don't like guns."

His life in law enforcement involved a lot of danger, a lot of guns and a lot of drama, too, although it was usually other people's drama. He stepped in to enforce the law, enforce order.

Now he was part of the drama.

"I don't like it much, either," he said, and he realized in that moment that he didn't just mean the drama. He was tired of people shooting at him. Tired of wondering when he'd die. Being a part of the Marshal Service with its unique and proud history had been a point of pride to him, but the purpose it had also given was tarnished now.

Justice, Integrity, Service. The Marshals' motto rang hollow. Marshals were supposed to be the good guys, not the bad.

Shocking, this feeling of wishing suddenly he had something else, some other reason to get up every day. Or maybe it was just good timing since his career might well be over.

Or maybe it was just the moment at hand. He'd get over it. If he proved what he believed, nailed the traitor in the Marshals, found Molly…

He would still have a career, still have a life.

Maybe. Or he'd die in the process. If he saved Molly, it would be worth it.

She set the gun on the dash. "You don't need that to kill me. You could kill me with your bare hands before I figure out which end is up. Thanks for the dramatic gesture anyway."

Did this mean she was ready to trust him? Or that she'd given up?

"I promise you I'm not driving you out in the country to hurt you or harm you in any way," he said. The Impala flew around a curve. "I'm trying to save your life. I'm trying to save Molly's life. Is there a back way to one of the main roads, without going through Haven?"

For a long moment, he wasn't sure she'd answer. Relief socked him when she spoke.

"Yes."

"How?"

She pointed to the road. "This is Showens Creek Road. If we keep going the way we were headed, take a couple of turns, it'll get us there eventually."

How much she trusted him, he still wasn't sure, but he had to get her to relax enough to tell him what she'd said in that interview with the Marshals. Then he'd stash her someplace safe and rescue Molly or die trying. As soon as he figured out what the hell the connection was between the threats to the judge, the mafia and someone inside the U.S. Marshals.

Someone who might or might not actually be his own commander….

Something had been in that outcome report from Marysia's interview. Something someone didn't want him to see. Probably something she didn't even understand, some clue that might not make sense to her but would to him, especially with what he'd already learned tonight. He had a feeling he was close. The pieces of the mystery roiled inside his head.

"Turn here," Marysia said when they came to another narrow road. "Then there's another low-water bridge, and after that there's a switchback to the right. If we take that, it goes over to Maple Ridge Road and runs into another road that goes to the main road and on to I-79. It'll take us to that exit that's about ten miles north of the Haven exit. The Bear Hill exit."

"How far from here?"

"Fifteen miles, I think."

Fifteen miles, he could do. He knew the exit off the interstate she was talking about. The town of Bear Hill was little more than a wide spot in the road, but the road was a regular two-lane highway and there was a gas station there.

They passed a low-water bridge and he took the next right. Trees swayed over the road. There were no houses, no farms. Nothing but wild woods all around and the possibility that he and Jimmy Guarino weren't the only ones who'd thought about the back way out of Haven. As dangerous as it could be to return to Haven, there was no certainty that searchers, both on the right and the wrong side of the law, weren't fanning out in force on the minor side roads now.

Searchers who knew these back roads better than he did. It wasn't just more mafiosos he was worried about. He didn't like to think about how easily local law enforcement would turn them over to the U.S. Marshals.

"Turn there," she said.

The Impala bounced over a rut in the road. It was unfamiliar territory to him and dark. And the gauge was sitting right above E.

Headlights came up behind them, more than one set. He picked out the dark shape of two SUVs.

Close. Too close. And fast.

He couldn't see the vehicles, couldn't tell if they were law enforcement—or something worse. More Jimmy Guarinos.

A shot shattered the rear window of the Impala and he decided *something worse* was the likely scenario. Marysia screamed as he floored it, careening around a sharp curve, desperate, driving like he knew these back roads. There would be no dealing with them this time. He was outnumbered.

Adrenaline, hard and heavy, rushed his veins.

"Hit the floor," he shouted at her, reaching over, shoving her head down when she didn't move immediately. Another shot came through the rear of the Impala, shattering the passenger-side window this time.

If he hadn't pushed her down when he had—

He took a turn wildly, heard her cry as she hit the passenger-side door where she huddled on the floor of the careening car. Gideon swore under his breath, focused, using sheer strength to handle the car as he took one wild curve after another, losing the tail, then finding them right back behind him. He took another turn, gunned it up a steep stretch, rounded a blind curve, then another.

A track appeared in his headlights and he shifted hard into lower gear, barreling the Impala up the rough, rutted path. A cemetery burst into view, ancient headstones tumbling over surrounded by a small chain-link fence.

He shut the lights and turned the car quickly in the tall weeds, the Impala pointed straight back down the hill in the dark.

"What are we doing?" Marysia's voice was a hoarse whisper.

He glanced down at her, caught her shining, horrified gaze.

"Losing 'em."

Her gulp of panic was audible.

Below, he saw one set of headlights, then two, appear through the trees on the road below, drive past, disappear, swallowed up in the thick night and lashing rain and wild turns.

He let the Impala creep back down the hill, hit the lights and turned back in the opposite direction.

Turned, then turned again. He didn't know where he was at this point and it didn't matter.

They thought he was heading for the interstate. They'd keep looking for him on every road out of here tonight.

And he didn't have enough fuel to keep outrunning them.

Marysia clambered back up to her seat, grabbing the dash, hanging on as he kept careening around curves.

"We lost them?" she breathed.

"Think so." Hoped so.

She was silent for a beat beside him. The wild woods spinning by outside the car seemed to close in on the road, close in on the car. Dark, ominous. Ready to swallow them whole.

"Where are we?" she asked.

The new panic poking through her voice had his adrenaline jolting up a few notches even as his options continued down the toilet. He hadn't wanted to hole up this close to Haven, but so be it.

"I don't have the slightest clue," he admitted. "But if we're lucky, and I think we're owed some luck, neither does anyone else."

Chapter 5

Lost. They were lost. And people kept shooting at them. Mary worked really hard at *not* having a full-blown panic attack.

He took another turn, hard.

She grabbed at the dash again, bracing herself. The car jerked over uneven asphalt. "So what are we going to do?"

"If we keep driving around, we're going to run out of gas before we find our way out of here," he said flatly.

"So what are we going to do?" she repeated. She needed a plan to hang on to. Step one, step two, step three.

"Wait for morning when we can see where the hell we're going."

"What are we going to do until morning?" Was that her voice? She swallowed over a quivering in her throat.

"Hole up."

Hole up? Was this actually her life, or was this one big freaky nightmare? This morning, she'd just been Mary O'Hurley, reclusive widow, planning to bake pie and watch TV. Tonight, she was the target of multiple killers for reasons she still didn't completely understand and on the run with a wildly sexy federal agent who was scaring the pants off her. And that was almost literal.

She would have laughed, but that was so not funny on more than one level. She'd been shot at three separate times, she couldn't go home and she had the audacity to think *sex* every time she looked at Gideon Brand. Her life was off the charts.

He turned the Impala up another overgrown trail. It was barely wide enough for a vehicle. An old oil road, maybe, but she discovered when they rounded the bend in the rough drive that it stopped at a cabin nearly hidden in overgrowth.

He cut the engine.

"Proof we're in luck," he said. "What do you think?"

"I don't think I'm feeling real lucky."

"You're still alive," he pointed out.

Yeah, there was that.

The rain slowed, still tapping on the car. The night loomed in misty uncertainty around them. She looked at the man beside her. Her gaze locked with his warily. Damp hair tangled wildly around her neck and she reached up, pulled at the sticky mess of it.

His face seemed carved out of stone, his eyes shadowy yet blade-sharp, tempered steel. Tempered by hell, she sensed suddenly. She saw, again, pain etched in those intense eyes of his. She had to fight, and fight hard, the energy that slammed into her when she looked at him.

She jerked the track of her mind away from such dangerous material, inspected herself instead. She was a mess.

Her clothes, denim capris and a once-pale yellow sleeveless button-down top, were soaked to her skin, ripped and muddy. She was uncomfortable, scared, lost.

And now stuck here. In the middle of nowhere. Until daylight.

With six feet of big, bad sexy male.

Some women would definitely label that last bit lucky. She found it terrifying.

"You doing okay?" he asked.

He was looking at her with such focus she could feel his hot gaze scorching her all the way to the tips of her toes. She couldn't possibly look remotely attractive, and yet she felt a weird lump in her throat. He didn't find her attractive. She was being an idiot.

Even her own husband hadn't found her attractive on a good day, and this was not a good day. And Gideon Brand was out of her league, way out, on her best day.

"I'm fine," she lied. "I'm sorry for causing so much trouble." He *had* been saving her life, and if it hadn't been for her, maybe they'd have gotten away without nearly getting killed.

"I'm sorry about running low on gas. We should have been better prepared for people to start shooting at us today."

Ha-ha. So he had a sense of humor.

She knew this whole situation wasn't funny, though. "You said there's not much time. For Molly. And now we're stuck here."

"No, there's not much time. Seventy-two hours to be precise. And the first twenty-four are fast slipping away. But I was stuck before we got here, Marysia. I need information."

Right. Back to that. He thought she knew something.

"I hope you don't think I can take you to Molly because I can't."

"Not yet."

"You're wasting your time. You're wasting Molly's time. I don't know what your other options are, but any of them are better than counting on me."

He shook his head. "I don't think so."

"I told you—"

"You're not a psychic, I heard that." He let a beat draw out. "Let's say you're not, if that makes you more comfortable. But someone thinks you are."

"Who?"

"Someone in the Marshal Service."

Confusion warred with the nerves jangling inside her. "I still don't understand that."

"You were interviewed by someone in the Marshals. About Flight 498." When she didn't say anything, he prompted, "You made a call to the airport that day, to the police. You warned them that the plane was going to explode."

"Sometimes even crackpots are right," she said thinly, transferring her attention to the window.

The cabin loomed against the stormy sky. It was set up on a hill, surrounded by trees. Maybe dappled in sunlight, it was cheerful, but tonight it just looked creepy.

Did he think they were spending the night inside that cabin? West Virginia was an outdoor recreation state. Hunting and fishing cabins dotted every rural road, standing unattended by their out-of-state owners the majority of time. It was small, the usual size for hunting cabins in these parts. In the car beams, she could see log siding and a narrow front porch. It didn't look like anyone had used it lately based on its unkempt state, overgrown with vines.

What was he planning to do, break in?

"What made you make those calls?" he asked.

"Hysteria."

"Okay. That's one possibility." He sounded patient, annoyingly so, as if she were a stubborn child. "That's what the authorities assumed when they received your calls. It's not the only possibility. Do you know that at one time you were considered a suspect, checked out thoroughly to determine whether you might have had any involvement in the bombing?"

That got her attention.

"No, I didn't know that!"

He shrugged. "You were easily dismissed as a viable person of interest. Small town piano teacher, no criminal record, no known connections to illegal activity. A psychic in her spare time at fairs and school carnivals."

"A *pretend* psychic."

"You believed it was real that day or you wouldn't have called. You convinced yourself since then that you were hysterical. But you believed in yourself that day, didn't you?"

The rain stopped completely. His words were scaring her, as much as those shooters had.

"Why don't you believe in yourself now, Marysia?"

She turned her head, stared at him in the darkness.

"Thirty-four people died on that plane," she said sharply. "I saw it blow up! But I was too late. I didn't save any of those people. I didn't save Danny." Her throat tightened as if a fist squeezed it.

"Do you think that was your fault?"

She flinched at that. She wanted to tell him to leave her alone, but her vocal cords didn't want to cooperate.

"It's not that you don't believe in yourself, is it?" he kept on. "It's that you think you screwed up. You think you should have seen it sooner. Or should have made someone believe you. Something. If you admit, even to yourself, that you really are psychic, then you'd have to admit that it was all your fault. Or at least that's how you see it. Maybe that's how you want to see it. Maybe you feel sorry for yourself."

A flash of anger, blessed anger, smacked her in the gut.

"Is that your official conclusion?" As if he knew her. As if he had any right to psychoanalyze her.

"Not yet. I'm waiting for confirmation."

She couldn't think of anything to say, or at least anything that was appropriate. She pushed out of the car, slammed the passenger door behind her.

Wind rattled the trees. Over the storm's remnants, over the roar of anger and hurt inside her head as she stomped toward the cabin, she heard another car door slam. He was coming after her.

Of course. He was relentless. He thought she knew something and he was going to take her head apart to find it. She wanted to run straight into the woods, but she knew that was stupid.

The cabin wasn't much more enticing. When she was a kid, her family vacationed at a cabin every summer. She and her sister would climb trees, swing on grapevines, skip rocks. It had been fun, except for the mice scurrying under the beds at night.

She climbed the steps. The wooden boards creaked but held. She tried the door. It was locked. She turned, looked for Gideon Brand.

He was nowhere to be seen. He'd shut the headlights and there was nothing but thick darkness around her now. A deer huffed in the woods. She shivered in the muggy night despite its warmth.

Where was he? She should have been relieved he wasn't right on top of her, invading her space, but perversely, she felt abandoned. Didn't he know she was scared to death? Just because she didn't want to speak to him, that didn't mean she wanted to be left alone.

What if she needed more lifesaving?

A sound came from around the side of the cabin. Panic jerked through her bloodstream but before she could formulate rational thought, a ray of light struck her face then dropped, revealing Gideon Brand behind it, coming up around the corner of the cabin.

"There you are. I was—" Scared. She stopped mid-blurt. She stared at her feet, sucking in a badly-needed lungful of air.

The Maglite he'd gotten from somewhere—the car, she supposed—bounced bright gold circles as he took the steps in what seemed like a single bound. Action movie hero, back on the set.

She just didn't want him to know that she'd missed him.

His eyes flickered in the shadows.

"I was just checking around the back. I'm not going to disappear on you. Don't worry."

"I'm not worried." Embarrassment soaked her voice. Why did he look so big on the cabin porch? He was supposed to occupy less space out of the car than in it.

He tried the door, then took something out of his jeans.

"Hold this here." He handed her the flashlight.

She pointed it at the door as he directed and watched as he flipped open what looked like an ordinary pocketknife but clearly wasn't. He did something to the lock and, voilà, turned the knob.

"How'd you do that?" she asked.

"F.M."

"What?"

He took the flashlight back and swung it around inside.

"Not bad," he said without answering her question. "Come on."

She felt light-headed. Everything about this night was too surreal. She stepped inside the cabin, brushing past him.

He was right. It wasn't bad. The neglected exterior

belied the cabin's cozy tidiness. The owners probably visited little more than a handful of times per year, but as was often the case, the cabin appeared fully supplied and appointed. There was a rag rug in blues on the wood plank floor. A scattering of worn furniture gathered facing a stone hearth. The kitchen was simple but serviceable. A double bed sat in one corner, with a chest beside it, and the opposite wall held twin bunks.

Room for the whole little hunter-gatherer family. Kerosene lamps sat in key positions around the room.

And it was *one* room. One big room.

Minus a bathroom.

"There's an outhouse in the back," he said.

"Oh, goody," she replied. "I was hoping for that."

She'd been thirteen the last time she'd seen the inside of an outhouse. There had always been a spider in it.

She watched him light the kerosene lamps with matches he took off the stone mantel. The kerosene was low in all the globes, but there was enough for a few hours.

He finished lighting the lamps and stood there, seconds ticking by, staring at her. She swallowed down an unreasonable quivering in her throat. She was frantically conscious of his scrutiny, as if his eyes were connected to every nerve ending on her body.

"Are we safe here?" Her voice shook stupidly.

"Maybe."

"Oh. Thanks for the reassurance."

He picked up the flashlight from the mantel where he'd set it. "I'm going back outside. I need to check the car."

"Check the car for what?"

"Tracking devices."

Her stomach dropped. She didn't know what to say. Screaming seemed like it might feel good.

"I'll be back," he said. "Don't go anywhere."

She watched him go outside, shutting the cabin door behind him. Why was he so calm? His steadiness should have made her feel better, but it was freaking her out. She was starting to think he'd stand calmly while the whole world blew up around him. She had no idea how to tell when things were really bad.

What she needed was a threat level system—yellow, orange, red….

Following after his big, bad ultra-competence was tempting. She was way out of her element with him. He was definitely threat level red.

What were they going to do if there was a tracking device on his car? Did he know how to remove it? Stupid question.

Supercop was probably out there right now chewing it off with his teeth and spitting it out.

And what was she doing? Running and hiding, literally and figuratively. She couldn't handle her own screwed-up head, much less a killer. *If you admit,*

*even to yourself, that you really are psychic, then
you'd have to admit that it was all your fault.*

She was startled to feel something wet and hot on
her face. She was crying, dammit. She scrubbed at
her face with her palms. So maybe Gideon Brand
was right. Maybe she blamed herself for what had
happened to that planeload of people, blamed herself
for not stopping it.

The tears fell harder. Yeah, she was screwed up all
right. She didn't want to be responsible for anyone
or anything. If she got involved, she'd just make
things worse. People would die.

Better, far better, to decide she couldn't help. She
was just a nutcase anyway.

Wow.

She had her free pass all lined up, didn't she?
Crazy was very liberating.

But assuming everything he'd told her was true,
just where did that leave a missing six-year-old girl
who could be murdered in less than three days?

The door opened and she made a last hard, fast
swipe at her cheeks. Not that his laser-piercing eyes
missed anything.

"You okay?" he asked, his gaze tight on her but
kind, shockingly kind.

Too kind. She couldn't take it. Especially from
big, bad supercop. If he offered a crumb of sympathy,
she'd dissolve into a puddle.

A guilty, cowardly puddle.

"Fine." She took a deep breath. *Coward.* That was definitely the right word. She was a coward. She'd been running and hiding, not just tonight but for a long time now. "What about— Did you find anything?"

He shook his head. "Nope."

She sniffed, blinked. God, she was scared, more scared than when bullets had been flying at her.

"So we're safe? What if they find us again?"

"They aren't going to find us tonight. There are roads twisting all over the place, not to mention abandoned oil field tracks shooting off everywhere. You can't see this cabin from the road. They aren't going to find us here. They don't even know we turned around."

"Okay. Good. Umm…"

He watched her, waiting for her to go on. Her chest felt tight and the suffocating feeling she was fighting threatened to overwhelm her. She straightened her spine, willed herself to speak past the huge ball of panic in her throat. She didn't want to be a coward.

"Maybe," she said, "you could tell me about Molly."

Chapter 6

Molly had four imaginary friends. She liked peanut butter and banana sandwiches and she had thirty-two stuffed horses, in all sizes and colors. She was an only child and had been living with her grandfather at his estate in Charleston since the judge's daughter had passed away after a short bout with cancer. Her father traveled extensively as vice president of a resort properties corporation and was currently out of the country.

"She went to bed last night at ten. The judge's home was gated and secured. There was no sign of entry or exit from the home, no obvious breach in security. No alarm activated. And yet at approximately 6:20 this morning, her bed was discovered empty. The judge had round-the-clock protection, but the agent on the scene overnight saw and heard nothing. I was in charge of supervising the protective detail and I was at the home myself this morning when she was found missing. Whether she was taken during the night, or early this morning, no one knows."

Gideon watched Marysia's ashen face, her eyes wide and brimming with tears she wouldn't shed. He'd coaxed her into sitting down in one of the worn but comfortably overstuffed armchairs in front of the cabin's cold stone hearth.

"It had to have happened fast," he went on. "And it had to have been well-planned. Whoever took Molly was able to bypass the security in place on the scene. Either they had the technological capacity to override it or they possessed the necessary information to access it."

He and the men under him on the detail knew the codes, as did Darren Tucker. But the showdown with Jimmy Guarino made it clear the mafia was involved in this thing somehow.

"And this is connected to the bombing how?"

He could almost hear her holding her breath, waiting for him to continue.

"Reinhold was due to take Flight 498, but he never boarded. With his work on the federal bench, the investigation into the bombing has centered around a possible attempt on the judge's life. Someone wants Reinhold off the bench. That's clear in the e-mail message he received after Molly's kidnapping. Both the bombing and the kidnapping appear to be targeting the same result, making it even more likely they are connected."

"Can't e-mail be traced?"

"Usually. This was heavily encrypted with technology that allowed it to bypass central servers and erase itself within hours."

"How is the mafia involved?"

"This is organized crime out of Pennsylvania. The Pittsburgh mafia expanded its territory over the years to include parts of Ohio and West Virginia. Illegal gambling, drugs, racketeering and everything that goes with it. Successful prosecutions brought it to its knees in the past couple of decades, but it's back on the rise here with a new local crime boss named Nicholas Venezia. The Feds are turning up the heat again, particularly in West Virginia where the politicos are out to prove that bringing legalized gaming resorts to this area isn't endangering the public by an equal increase in illicit activity."

"And how did you know that guy back there was with the mafia?"

"Knowing the names and faces of every known member of the Pittsburgh crime family, particularly the West Virginia branch, is part of my job. His name was Jimmy Guarino. And believe me, if I had not shot him when I did, you and I would not be sitting here now. Or anywhere."

He gave her a second to absorb that.

"Judge Reinhold oversees wiretaps, secret grand jury testimonies," he explained. "Bribery's the mafia's best bet at beating justice. If the judge isn't playing, they'd have reason to want him off the bench. Kidnapping's up their alley, too, but we've never been able to connect them to the bombing. Attacks on airplanes aren't their style, though."

Now that he knew at least one federal agent was involved, he was starting to think that that individual was a much more likely culprit in the bombing. How it all tied together was still a mystery.

"Yesterday," he went on, "I requested all the interview outcomes that were taken after Flight 498. I decided to go back, start over, review every document. I got everything I asked for—except the one on you. Next thing I knew, I was relieved of duty, sent home on forced leave. Later, I discovered my phone was tapped."

Marysia sat very still, listening intently, her eyes bright in her pale face. She looked impossibly innocent and beautiful, and for a second it almost destroyed him to think how much danger she was in. Tomorrow, first thing, he would find someplace safe for her to ride this out.

He worked to focus on what he had to do tonight. "I went back to headquarters tonight. I logged in to the network and found your interview tracking ID was gone. Someone shot at me inside the building. Inside headquarters. And that same person or some-one working with him came here tonight, to Haven. Along with their backup, apparently."

"And you think those other SUVs, the ones chasing us—"

"Most likely Jimmy Guarino's friends. Could be other law enforcement agents involved with the mafia, too. How deep Venezia's in the Marshals, I don't know. Either way, there's no doubt now that someone inside the U.S. Marshals is working with the mafia. Law enforcement on the take is a chronic problem in prosecuting organized crime."

That Venezia could have a hold on someone as high as Tucker…. It was unbelievable, but he was starting to believe it.

"And whoever they are, they want me dead." She met his gaze with a directness, a fierceness, that showed both her fear and her strength. "You *did* save my life. More than once."

"It's my job."

"Will you still have a job when this is over?"

"Maybe. If I can save Molly. If I can find the traitor, or traitors, in the Marshals." If he lived. Adding that point was unnecessary.

He could see the shadow of anxiety in her eyes. She knew too well by now how much danger they were in.

She chewed at her lower lip for a moment. There

was a leaf in her hair, mud on her cheeks. She was a mess, an absolute mess, and yet still lovely. No makeup and no need for it. Clothes ripped and wet and dirty.

He felt a spear of guilt. He'd pushed her hard and she was cooperating now. She'd already been through a lot tonight. It was time to let up on the pressure for a bit or he'd risk her cracking.

"There might be some clothes in that chest over there," he said. "You need to get out of those wet things. I'll see if I can dig up something to eat." Then he'd push her again, hard, about Flight 498. In the meantime, he'd get his head straight that she was just part of the job.

She blinked. "Uh—"

She looked around, back at him.

"It's okay. I won't peek." He watched her flush prettily. What he wouldn't give to peek. Dammit. "Or you can change in the outhouse."

That distracted her. "In the dark?"

He handed her the flashlight. She took it warily, looked down at her soaked, muddied clothes again, seemed resigned.

The chest yielded a variety of camouflage gear in youth and adult sizes. She picked out a camo T-shirt and drawstring pants, while he found a can of chili in the cabinet and lit the woodstove. There was a small pile of leftover kindling inside.

"Scream if you want me to kill a spider for you," he offered.

She gave him a narrow look. "I don't think so."

He pushed back a tantalizing image of her careening naked out of the outhouse, into his arms. Yep, he was definitely having a problem not noticing her as a woman.

Work on it, he reminded himself.

He stood in the back doorway of the cabin, watching her as she disappeared into the outhouse, waiting for her until she emerged, looking shockingly sexy in camo. The T-shirt, even dry, clung to her curves and the drawstring pants accentuated her small waist and far-too-appealing hips.

"You didn't have to stand guard," she said.

He shrugged. "No spiders?" It hadn't really been spiders he'd been worried about. He felt they were safe for now, but he wasn't taking anything for granted. He wasn't leaving her alone outside.

"None I couldn't handle," she said.

She tipped her chin, and damn, she was sexy. In the face of everything that had happened, and everything still ahead, she was trying to find her ground, be strong.

"What about you?" she went on. "Aren't you going to change? There are plenty of clothes. Or are you the one who's afraid of spiders? There was a big one in there, just so you know. Oh, wait, I forgot, nothing scares you."

There was a bitterness to her tone he didn't understand.

"I don't know what makes you think that," he

said, not liking the thread of bitterness in his own tone. "I'm scared of a lot of things, Marysia."

He turned away, from her and from the moment, the moment that was too dangerous in too many ways, and grabbed some clothes for himself. In the back of one of the drawers, he spotted a map of abandoned oil field roads in the area, a typical tool hunters used to negotiate the backwoods. Maybe, just maybe, it could be their safe way out. He'd need daylight, though.

"I feel bad about taking these clothes," she said.

He glanced back at her from the door. "I left a couple of bills in the drawer," he said.

"Oh. Okay. I'll put something in there, too. I'll get my purse."

"I left enough."

She ignored him and went for her purse anyway. Stubborn, she was. He went on to the outhouse and changed quickly. By the time he got back, she'd set out bowls of chili, two, across the table from each other. Quite the little domestic scene.

Her gaze lowered as he walked in. Already seated, she toyed with the spoon, clearly tense. He wasn't comfortable, either. When was the last time he'd sat down to dinner with a beautiful woman?

Well, okay, about four months ago, which was evidently too long ago to keep his libido under control if his reaction to Marysia was any indication. Her name had been Sandra and he'd slept with her. She didn't expect anything from him, which was why he'd picked her.

Marysia O'Hurley was the kind of woman who'd expect something. He had no business thinking about her that way.

"Thanks," he said, seating himself across from her. He took a bite. She still didn't eat.

"I'm not really hungry," she said finally. Her earnest gaze hit him dead-on. "Just tell me what to do to help Molly."

He considered her for a long moment. He'd been prepared to push her, but she was offering herself up voluntarily.

"You tell me. How does it usually work, the psychic thing?"

"Usually? What usually?" She pushed back her chair, drew her knees up and wrapped her arms around her legs. Fetal position, almost. She so didn't want to have this conversation—and yet she seemed eager to be done with it. "I used to do the carnival thing, mostly for the local school, sometimes for fairs. Reading palms, crystal ball and people's auras. Just silly stuff." She hesitated, as if she had to steel herself to go on.

"Maybe I had what people call natural psychic abilities. I didn't take them seriously. My grandpa died when I was little and I used to think I could communicate with him. Supposedly artistic people are more prone to feeling their natural psychic abilities, but probably that's just our natural instability."

She gave a brittle laugh, then her look turned pensive. He didn't like how she put herself down.

"What happens to me now, or what I think sometimes happens," she continued, "would fall into what is supposedly a form of sensory projection—sensing energies, emotions of other people, usually people I'm familiar with or sometimes events in places I'm familiar with. It's not something that happens when I touch someone or touch something that belongs to them. I have to be familiar, somehow, with the people or the place to feel the energies and emotions. Or maybe I'm just a highly imaginative wacko!"

"Stop calling yourself crazy," he said, angry—not at her, but for her, for how she felt about herself.

She squeezed her eyes shut for a moment, blew out a ragged breath. "I'm just trying to be rational about it."

"Doesn't that prove you're not crazy?" he asked. "That you can be rational about it?"

The moment stretched long, tight. He wondered, suddenly, if she sensed anything about him. The thought was sharply uncomfortable. He was a closed book to other people and he liked it that way. People who'd known him long enough knew about the divorce, about what had happened to Lizzie.

And they knew better than to bring up any of it. He had places inside him too dark to go.

Hell, yes, Marysia O'Hurley was wrong if she thought nothing scared him.

Her voice broke into his thoughts as she went on.

"Everything changed after the earthquake," she was saying. "You know about the Haven earthquake, what people said about Haven?"

"Flashes of light, positive ions triggering paranormal activity, etcetera, yes, I saw the news," he said.

"Most people just, you know, blew it off." Her voice trailed off.

"You?"

"Mostly," she said. "I saw these weird lights that night, the ones people talked about on the news. Red lights, horizontal. I was out on the back porch of our house when the quake hit. It was like those lights went straight through me."

She pushed back the still-damp hair that fell forward across her cheek, tucked it behind her ear.

"It was very strange," she said, "and there was a lot of hysteria in town. There had been a lightning storm that night. I figured I'd imagined the whole thing. I was freaked out, like everybody else. Then this neighbor, Patsy Renniker, came over after the earthquake and I just knew she had cancer. As soon as I looked at her, I could feel the disease inside her. It scared the crap out of me. I never did another reading after that. I told Patsy to go to the doctor."

"Did she?"

"Not then. She was really upset with me for giving her a reading like that. But then she found a lump and went in for a mammogram. She had cancer."

"You probably saved her life," he said. "Even if it took a while for her to check it out."

Her gaze turned overbright. "No, she died."

"That wasn't your fault."

"Patsy had told people what I said, that she should go see a doctor. Then there was the whole thing after the plane blew up. The media circus started up again, and it got so bad that I couldn't even answer my phone. I canceled all my appointments with my students. I was depressed, anyway," she said in a flip way that wasn't really flip at all. "I just feel crazy sometimes."

She jerked her gaze away from him, her voice thready. "And most people, rational people, thought I was crazy. They treated me as if I was the one trying to make something of it. And then when the plane exploded… The media circus over the earthquake and that paranormal detective on the news… It all just turned into a big joke, and I felt like the punch line."

"I don't think you're crazy."

"You're not inside my head!" She put a trembling hand to her lips. "That morning…" she blurted, her voice going painful, "I could see Danny sitting on the plane. See the people surrounding him, hear snatches of their conversations, flashes of their thoughts. It was like I knew all about them, every one of them. And then I knew they were going to die."

She was dancing around the details still. He

waited, knowing if he pushed her now, she'd fall apart. He had to give her whatever time she needed. She got up, walked around as if she couldn't sit still.

He could see her wipe surreptitiously at her eyes. She didn't want him to know she was crying.

"That had to have been awful."

"It was awful for them, not me," she said roughly, her shining eyes stabbing him now. She stopped in front of the kitchen counter. It was made of butcher block and there was a metal rooster sitting in one corner, the lone decor. The kerosene lamp he'd set on the table burned low, casting shadows and light across her haunted face. "It wasn't me on that plane."

"You had to see it, and you didn't want to see it," he said, rising. "And you weren't responsible for what happened, you know. You did everything you could."

"Now there's Molly," she said. "If it's even real, I would help you find Molly if I could. I hardly remember the day they interviewed me about the plane. I don't know what I said that would make anyone want me dead now, what they wouldn't want you to know. All I can do is tell you what I saw, because that's all I told them."

"That's all I can ask," he said.

"I don't want to be a coward," she whispered brokenly, suddenly. "I don't want to run and hide when there's a little girl out there who could die."

Her shoulders shook and she buried her face in her

hands. As much as he knew she didn't want to, she was openly crying now.

He didn't even think. He went to her, wrapped his arms around her.

She thought she was a coward. That killed him. That's why she'd changed her mind, decided to voluntarily talk to him about Molly and the plane crash and the psychic ability she didn't want to face.

"You are not a coward," he told her. He heard her choked sob against his chest. She pulled back, lifted her tear-streaked face. "You're a strong, beautiful woman, Marysia."

He hadn't meant to tell her she was beautiful.

There was shock in her eyes, maybe a flicker of panic. Shock and panic that reverberated inside him. Seconds of charged awareness ticked by.

Seconds that felt like hours. And he knew—God, he knew—she felt it, too. She knew it, too. She *knew* he wanted to…kiss her.

And it was like that damn earthquake. He knew nothing else was ever going to be the same.

Chapter 7

Bolt. Scream. Spin around and run for your life. All those options bounced wildly through Mary's mind, but she couldn't move or speak. Gideon Brand reached up, pushed back an unruly curl from her cheek.

He wanted to kiss her.

She felt her nipples, taut against the camo T-shirt, pebbling with need. She terrified herself. *He* terrified her, the energy she could read from him all too well. His eyes locked with hers, and she was keenly aware of his arm still around her, his hand touching her face.

His hard, gorgeous mouth was right there, so close. She could see him dipping his face down, putting his lips to hers.

She *wanted* him to do that. She wanted to make love to him, just the way she'd imagined. No, the way she'd *foreseen* it.

Her heart thudded against her ribs and heat vibrated low in her body. All he was doing was *looking* at her and her thighs were shaking, her pulse fluttering in frantic anticipation. She wanted to tip herself right into a wild, breathless fantasy, past the point of no return, free fall straight into this night the way she had foreseen it.

Panic reared its head.

Holy cow, one teeny bit of flattery and she puddled. There was a place for cowardice, and it was here. She reached between them, pushed the flat of her palm against his rock-hard chest.

What was wrong with her? Was it too many months of sleeping alone?

Too many nights sleeping alone even before Danny had died. The secret unhappiness in their marriage. The passion she'd always longed for but never known. And why did she think she'd find it now, in the arms of a total stranger?

Perspective! Killers were after her! After them both! Not to mention an innocent six-year-old child. And she was a widow, with a husband not even gone a year. Talk about inappropriate! That their marriage hadn't been worth mourning a month, that wasn't the point. Danny had been a human being. He'd been her husband. If she'd divorced him the way she'd intended, that would be one thing. But their marriage hadn't ended in divorce. It had ended in his death.

"I— This—" She couldn't form a coherent sentence to save her life.

Gideon's gaze followed her as she practically jumped away from him. His energy was so clear to her one minute then absolutely inscrutable the next. He appeared, as usual, in perfect control of himself even as sexual heat pulsed off him in waves. She had no idea what he was thinking.

"I'm sorry. I didn't mean to fall apart there." Finally, she managed to put a sentence together even as she shook limply all over. Fear, it hit her suddenly. Fear stopped her cold.

"You didn't fall apart," he said. "You're still standing here."

She shrugged. "Yeah."

Standing here. With her wits scattered all over the floor and a stunning realization that she needed more time to sort out.

His gaze sifted into her as if making its way straight into her mind, her fantasies, her thoughts. She could almost believe *he* was the one with the so-called psychic ability.

He was a trained law enforcement officer. He was probably damn good at reading people, no superpowers required.

Scary, that.

She swallowed hard.

"You're standing here and you're trying to help," he went on. "I think you're being pretty brave, Marysia. Courage isn't the absence of fear, you know. Courage is what happens in its presence."

She wondered what he'd meant earlier when he'd said he was scared of many things. And maybe… Maybe if she stopped being so scared of him, she'd know….

Slamming down on that dangerous idea, she said the first thing that popped into her head.

"Could you call me Mary? I keep thinking my mother's talking to me when you call me Marysia." That was a lie, except for the part where it was only her mother who called her Marysia.

She definitely didn't think about her mother when she looked at Gideon Brand.

"Okay. Mary."

Now that sounded too familiar and she wished she'd done something other than babble that inanity at him.

She sat back down at the table and he followed suit. Brave. Yeah, it was time to be brave. Too bad she didn't feel brave, but she could fake it. Somehow, she wanted to live up to his praise, stupid as that was, and for sure she needed to stop thinking about kissing him and whether he wanted to kiss her.

The kerosene lamp spilled a glow that spread to shadows. She stared down at the scarred wood and made herself start talking.

"I called the airport that morning and they put an airport cop on the line. I told him I thought something was going to happen to that plane. It was going to blow up. I told them my husband was on board, and he asked me if I was scared of flying. The officer took my name and number and thanked me. I knew he didn't believe me. I called the city police and I told them, too. I kept trying to call Danny, but he had his cell phone turned off."

The interview. That was what he wanted to know about. She went on. "It was the next day when two U.S. Marshals came to the door. There were a lot of people in the house, because of Danny. He was a coach at the high school, so my family, his family, our friends, teachers from school—" And she'd only wished they'd all go away, leave her alone. But they'd helped, too. Fielding phone calls from the media who didn't seem to care that her husband had just died, just wanted to pepper her with questions about the calls she'd made to the airport and the police. Somehow the information had gotten out. It had been one big nightmare.

"I'm sorry about your husband, Mary."

She stomped down on the hollow feeling that threatened to consume her. Truth came out of her mouth. Truth she'd never told anyone.

"Our marriage was over. We were going to get divorced."

His eyes seemed very deep suddenly. "Then it was

a double loss for you, wasn't it? You'd already lost the marriage. I'm sure you still cared about your husband."

"Yeah." She didn't know what to think of his reaction. It was as if he understood. Of course, he'd known loss, terrible loss, too. He'd told her he'd lost a friend on Flight 498.

"I need to know what made you make those calls," he said. "What you told the Marshals."

She took a deep breath, steeled herself.

"I could see Danny in the passenger lounge, waiting to board the plane. I've been to that airport lots of times, of course. I was just thinking about him, that's all. That's what I figured. I could imagine him there, in the passenger lounge. I looked at the clock in the kitchen and knew he'd probably be boarding soon. It was an early flight and I hadn't even gotten up before he left for Charleston. He'd left coffee on for me and I was pouring a cup.

"Then it was like I could hear him talking to the woman sitting next to him, just chitchat. I knew he was getting in line to board and I could see him sitting down in his seat after he stowed his carry-on. I was washing up some dishes I'd left in the sink from the night before, just thinking about Danny. He'd applied for a coaching job at a small college in Maryland and we'd argued about it. That's why he was flying to D.C., for the interview. I didn't want to move, and that's when—"

She looked outside now, at the window over the

kitchen sink. That's when she'd told him she wanted a divorce. She didn't say it, didn't have to. She looked back at Gideon, saw the knowing in his eyes.

"There was this baby," she said. "Crying and crying, and it wouldn't stop. The mom was trying so hard. The stewardess came by and tried to help. This older man was asking for a pillow and a blanket and I knew he had just retired. His wife was sitting next to him and she was reading a book about traveling to Europe on a budget. She was excited. I could *feel* how excited she was. They were making a connection in D.C. to London.

"It was so weird. I remember thinking, what is going on? I wasn't scared, though. Not then. I tried to call Danny and I realized he must have already turned his phone off. I didn't connect it to what had happened to me after the earthquake or to the thing with Patsy Renniker. I didn't think this was anything… Anything abnormal. I thought I was just thinking about Danny and other times when I'd been on planes, and… I don't know. I could just see all these people on the plane with him, like I was there and I knew a piece of their stories. I figured it was random memories mixing together with my thinking about Danny going to D.C."

She got up out of her seat, the energies of all those people pounding through her. She couldn't sit still. Every bit of the sensory projection of that fatal day rushed her.

Words tumbled out, one after another, as she told him about other people on that flight. She paced, turned, paced some more.

"There was this guy, a cop or something— Oh, my God." She stopped short, locking her gaze with his. "He was a U.S. Marshal. He was your friend. I'm so sorry." She felt Gideon's energy sharply now, felt his pain.

"Please go on," he said tightly. "I don't want you to stop."

She bit her lip, nodded, working to push away the pain emanating from him so she could continue. "He was sitting next to Danny and he was talking on his cell phone, arguing with somebody about how he had no business going to D.C. now and he wanted to get off the plane. Whoever he was talking to was ordering him to take the flight anyway and he didn't understand why."

Gideon's energy changed, grew hot somehow, but she was caught up in her own heartbreak now.

"I could see the ground crew outside on the tarmac," she whispered. "I could see someone driving by outside the plane window with a baggage cart. I remember wishing Danny hadn't already turned his phone off. They hadn't taken off yet. I wanted to tell him I was sorry that we'd argued and that I hoped he got the job in Maryland, that I hoped he would be happy. I didn't want everything to end so bitterly. Then suddenly— It was like every heartbeat stopped.

They were going to die. There was going to be an explosion. I saw the fire. I saw them all dead.

"I tried to call Danny. I tried and tried. I called the police. The plane hadn't taken off yet. I had to stop it. I was terrified." The anguish doubled her over.

Strong arms wrapped her from behind.

"I couldn't stop it!"

Gideon's arms pulled her around, pulled her up. She buried her face in his shirt. She didn't care if she was crying again. She sobbed like a baby and didn't care.

He held her, just held her, and she didn't want him to stop. She wanted to climb up his big, hard body, climb right into all the comfort he offered. She was shaking so hard, she could almost feel her teeth rattle.

The only thing holding her together was him. His heat, his strong arms.

He cupped her face then, tipped her gaze up to his even as he held her tightly still.

His eyes, tortured, held hers for an interminable beat. She couldn't pull away even though she suddenly had the brain power to know she should. She shouldn't be this close to him. And yet wasn't that the fear talking? The fear that had blocked her in so many ways, the fear that was holding her back from living her life again?

She was afraid of not being afraid.

"It's over," he said. "It's over. You did all you could."

"I didn't do anything."

"You tried. There was nothing else you could do, Mary."

She felt a bubble of hysteria rise in her throat and she struggled to control it. Was this how wild she'd been that day when she'd called the police? No wonder no one had listened to her.

"That's all I can remember," she told him shakily. She pushed away from him even though she could feel her knees wobbling. She had to be strong. "I'm sure that's what I told the Marshals. It's all I could have told them. I'm sorry. I know it doesn't help Molly."

Her chest wrenched. She couldn't do anything for those people on that plane, not then and not now. And she didn't have the slightest idea how anything she'd told the Marshals that day, and had told Gideon tonight, would help that little girl.

"You're wrong."

She blinked, stared at Gideon. She shivered as she took in the deadly hard expression that had taken over his eyes.

"What do you mean?"

Chapter 8

"You were right about the man sitting next to your husband. There was only one law enforcement officer on that plane that day and it was the federal agent who died. When the judge didn't make the flight, Robbie Buchanan had no reason to board. In fact, I ordered Buchanan to return to headquarters myself when I was notified that the judge hadn't made it to the airport. Tucker had reassigned Reinhold's driver that day and there was some mix-up, the driver didn't have the right information. I ordered Buchanan to leave the airport. Someone overrode my order. And that is what someone didn't want me to know."

Mary stared at him. "I could be wrong—"

"No," he said, hot emotion stabbing him. "I don't think you are."

It fit. Dammit, it fit.

Mary shook her head. "I don't understand." She was still trembling, badly.

He was just as shaken. And he had to take it all professionally. He couldn't lose it now. Molly needed him.

"Only one person could have overridden me and ordered Buchanan to board that flight, and to remain on board, when the judge didn't make it. The head of the U.S. Marshals' West Virginia judicial security division. Darren Tucker. The same person who was also responsible for Reinhold *not* making the flight."

Darren Tucker, who had said he had no idea why Buchanan remained on that flight. But that was a lie, had to be, and Tucker knew damn well that Gideon would question the strangeness of the order to Buchanan and the lie he'd told afterward. In the chaotic aftermath of the plane bombing, agents had been brought in from outside the judicial security division to take some of the interviews and Darren Tucker had assigned two of them to the psychic from Haven.

When Tucker became aware of what was in that file, he didn't know. The file could have been gone for months, but the entry in the databank had remained. A careless mistake on Tucker's part, most likely.

In his position, Tucker had nearly as much information as the judge. He didn't have the power, though. Buying information wasn't enough. The mafia would want to buy the power, too. And Tucker was helping them. He was a former military special ops hero. He would know how to blow up a plane.

And just what kind of pressure had that put on Reinhold, knowing Tucker had reassigned his driver, maybe given his driver the wrong information, kept the judge off that flight but with a powerful message.

Cooperate, or look what could happen. His life clearly in Tucker's manipulative hands. Tucker had to be on the take. And he'd wanted the judge in, too. Whether the judge wanted in or not. It made all the pieces fit. And it was uglier than he could have dreamed.

"Why?"

Hating the fear on her face, he stomped down on his own battle of emotions. "Maybe Buchanan was on the take along with Tucker and he got scared, wanted out. I don't know. Either way, he was disposable. When the judge realized he just barely missed a flight that would have killed him, he certainly would have had a second chance to consider his options with the mafia if Tucker let him know he'd arranged for him to miss it. It would certainly show the judge what could happen to him if he didn't start cooperating. Tucker could have threatened him.

"Maybe Reinhold even cooperated for a while, but stopped, who knows? They struck again. This time, they went after him through Molly."

Mary swallowed hard, wrapped her arms around herself. "So where is she?"

"It's highly unlikely Tucker has her. Or even that he took her. He's got a family. Wife, kids. And he's got friends, friends who owe him. Friends in the mafia. Holding Molly would be no problem for Nicholas Venezia."

"Who?"

"Head of the West Virginia branch of the Pittsburgh crime family."

"So you can take this theory and go to the authorities now? Right?"

He shook his head. "With what proof?" He had the testimony of a psychic.

The rest was coincidence without the missing piece Mary supplied. Even with that, it was a lot of conjecture. Conjecture that hit solid in Gideon's gut. He knew it was true, but his gut wasn't enough to send Tucker to jail. There had to be proof, somewhere, in Tucker's phone records, financial records. There had been a number of men who'd been unidentifiable in the security tapes of construction workers at the airport. Hard hats hiding most of their faces. With facial recognition software and a specific face to compare, that could change. They could look for Tucker now.

Putting Tucker under the heat lamp would be dangerous, though. Gideon didn't know who he could trust inside the Marshal Service, especially the local branch. He'd have to go straight to the top, to the director, but even then, it would take some time and talking to get anyone to listen to a Marshal who'd gone on the lam after pulling a gun on a guard at headquarters.

And once Venezia learned Tucker was in trouble, he'd get rid of Molly—probably at the bottom of a river.

"What are you planning to do?" Mary asked.

"Get you someplace safe for starters."

"What about you?"

"I'm not safe anywhere, Mary." Where would *she* be safe? She couldn't stay here. It was safe tonight, or as safe as he could find. Tomorrow, he'd have to do better. "But I can make sure you're safe."

He wanted her safe.

She tipped her chin at him. "I helped you. Now you're just— What? Done with me?"

"I don't want you hurt."

"What about you?" she cried. "You can't save the world by yourself! You need some kind of backup!"

"You can't be my backup, Mary. You're not qualified. You don't need to be involved in this anymore. And I'm not trying to save the world. I'm just trying to save one little girl."

"You just said you didn't have enough proof to go to the authorities—" She broke off with a gasp, eyes huge suddenly. "You're going to look for Molly. You're going to the mafia." When he didn't say anything, she charged on. "You can't do that! They'll kill you!"

"I'm not suicidal, Mary. I have a plan."

"Then tell it to me! Make me feel better!"

"I'm going to make a deal. You feel better now?"

"What kind of deal?"

"I'm going to give Venezia a chance to walk on the right side of the law for a change. If Tucker's cornered first, he'll bring Venezia down with him. I'm going to give Venezia the chance to do the right thing, and save his own skin in the process."

"You don't have the authority to make that deal."

"Tucker's bound to have been working with the mafia since before he brought down Flight 498, and any investigation into Tucker will lead to Venezia. If Venezia can strike first, pin that plane bombing on Tucker, his testimony is a deal no one in federal law enforcement is going to turn down. It's not a deal Venezia can turn down, either. If I go to Venezia before Tucker knows he's been made, then Venezia can save himself. His alternative would be to take more heat than any organized crime family has ever taken in history when he finds himself tangled up in an investigation into an airplane attack. He won't want that. In return, all I want is Molly."

"Are you out of your mind? He can just blow your head off! That would solve everything!"

"Not if I make a tape before I go to Venezia. A tape detailing everything I believe about Tucker, and mail it to the director of the U.S. Marshals—and the media. The director won't be able to turn a blind eye to what may sound unbelievable, not with the media on his tail. He'll have to investigate, and the truth *will* come out. Then Venezia goes down with Tucker."

"Then just do that now!"

"Molly would end up dead that way, Mary."

Silence, thick and heavy, pulled between them for a long beat.

"Molly could end up dead anyway. And so could you!"

"This is Molly's only chance."

"What about *your* life? How come you never seem worried about your own life? Why do you have to take everything on your own shoulders, alone? Why?"

"I'm doing my job."

"No, you're not!" she yelled at him, eyes flashing. "You were taken off the case, remember? But you're risking your life anyway. It's like it's almost personal."

He felt a hot ball of bitterness clog in his throat. Lizzie. Her little body so decomposed, only dental records identified her. Her murderer— Never captured. He pushed the anger down, feeling only the pain and anguish it left in its wake.

"If it is," he said carefully, "then it's none of your business."

Emotion charged the air. She turned her liquid eyes away from him, biting her lip. Feelings roiled

inside him, like an avalanche threatening to over-
power his common sense.

She turned, faced him again, and the hot, fierce
look in her eyes floored him. He heard a heartbeat.
Hers, his, he had no idea. She didn't look frightened
anymore, only angry.

"I see. I tell you everything, not just about Molly
but about me. And you—"

He felt the rapid-fire beat of his pulse. She'd given
him her trust, laid open her anguish and faced all her
fears, and he could give her nothing but goodbye. He
had nothing more to give.

"That was business," he said. "You don't need to
know anything more about me than you already know."

"Maybe I want to know!"

"That would be a very bad idea."

"Why is that? Do you feel responsible for Molly's
kidnapping? Do you feel guilty? Maybe you like
feeling sorry for yourself."

Seconds ticked by. She was throwing his words
back in his face. Oh yes, she was not afraid now.

And she wasn't done.

"Why are you afraid to tell me what makes this so
personal for you?" she charged on. "You told me you're
afraid of lots of things. Courage isn't the absence of
fear, you know. Courage is what happens in its presence. You said that. What are you afraid will happen if
you tell me why this is so personal for you, Gideon?"

"I'm asking you to back off, Mary."

Her determined eyes held him.

"Why? Am I one of those things you're afraid of? I am, aren't I? You're afraid to tell me anything that lets you get too close to me. I can cry on your shoulder and tell you everything, but you don't want to tell me anything except that you're planning to die."

"What do you want, Mary?" He stepped closer to her, looming over her. He wanted to intimidate her. Instead of being intimidated, she held her ground, tipped her chin at him again.

The oil flickered in the lamp in the sitting area. Flickered, then died. The lamp in the kitchen sputtered, signaling its own fading power.

"You saved my life. Maybe I want to save yours!"

"If you want to return the favor, then leave me alone."

"You don't do a very good robot impression, Gideon," she said. "I don't think—" Her voice wobbled and she did look scared again suddenly, then she pushed on fiercely, recovering. "I don't think you want me to leave you alone. I don't think you want to die. I think whatever is driving you, it *is* personal and it's emotional and if no one steps in and stops you, you're going to take risks you shouldn't take because of that emotion."

Gideon's chest clenched. His throat tightened and he felt tears heat his eyes. He wanted to detach from the depth of the pain and anguish he felt, but it was suddenly too strong.

"You had a little girl," Mary whispered starkly.

No. No, she couldn't know that.

"You had a little girl and she died. She was murdered. Oh, my God." She reached out, put her hand on his arm.

She knew. Of course she knew. He'd believed all along that she had some kind of psychic ability. She'd been scared of it, overwhelmed by it. And he'd talked her into facing it. She was sensing his emotions, reading his energy, seeing inside him.

He'd brought this on himself.

He closed his eyes, willed her to walk away, leave him alone.

"You have to save Molly because you couldn't save her," she persisted. "You couldn't save Lizzie."

She knew her name. His eyelids snapped up, and he saw the dampness of her eyes, the sudden shock shining out of them.

"I'm sorry," she whispered. "I'm so sorry, Gideon."

He meant to shake off her hand, but somehow he ended up taking hold of her instead.

"What do you want, Mary?" he asked her again, growling harshly. "Just want to know if you're right? Are you just curious?" Feelings raged inside him, flood waters about to roar over a dam. "Want to see if you've got your parlor trick down? You can go back to performing at school carnivals. You'll be a huge hit."

She flinched as if he'd struck her.

"Actually," she started, but her voice broke. She

stopped, cleared her throat. "I just wanted to be brave, because you made me believe I could be." She wiped at her eyes with her free hand, mopped the tears falling fast now. "Brave enough to know if what I knew about you all along was real. I'm sorry," she said again.

Guilt twisted through his pain and he had the clarity to know he'd been a complete bastard to her just now. She hadn't deserved it.

"No, I'm sorry. I don't want to hurt you, Mary," he whispered roughly, so torn up inside, he could hardly see straight. He had to make this pain stop, for her, for him. "That was uncalled for. I didn't mean that." He took a deep breath, his chest so tight he could hardly do it. "I know this is no parlor trick for you. You just need to understand that I have a job to do, personal or not, and if you knew all along about Lizzie, then you know that's not something I want to talk about."

"That's not what I meant." She looked so very serious, so strangely determined, a shadow of the old fear in her eyes but determination in her voice. Determination he didn't understand.

"Then what?"

And in that very long beat as he could almost see her overcoming that familiar fear, he knew it before she spoke. Not because he had any psychic power, but because it was all there, in her intensely blue eyes, eyes he knew, sharply knew, he could drown all those feelings in that were so out of control. Drown them not forever, but for at least one night. And knew, too, that it would be wrong, but that he needed it, needed her, and that he was way past caring that it was wrong because if he took what she offered he wouldn't feel as if he might explode in grief.

And somehow, shockingly, she needed him, too.

"I knew this." She tipped her face up to him, pressed herself against him as if she would die if he didn't fill her up, and she kissed him.

Chapter 9

Gideon's arms swooped around her, his mouth on her lips, her face, her neck. Liquid fire crashed through her veins, and she wasn't afraid. For the first time in so very long, she wasn't afraid. The impossible, the unbelievable, was about to happen.

She *wanted* it to happen.

No romantic expectations. Just fantasy, just need, just destiny. This night was meant to be. And after the drama she'd been through, tonight and for months before tonight, she deserved it.

And so did he. He was damaged, as damaged as she, and the two parts of them could make a whole. It was what they both needed. It was why they were here tonight. And if that was all just rationalizing what she wanted, she didn't care. Not tonight.

He pulled back, leaving her lips throbbing, her body pulsing, her breaths coming in sharp gasps, and their eyes locked. Everything else but him faded into some meaningless blur. She ached for him to touch her, take her.

And then he kissed her again, and it was as if even those few seconds apart had been a lifetime, she had missed him so much. He pulled her close, crushing his mouth to hers, his hard chest against her soft breasts. She ran her fingers through his hair, down his back, feeling as if she couldn't get enough of him, barely able to resist the urge to climb right inside his clothes.

He swept his hands to the curve of her bottom, breaking the kiss and gazing straight into her soul, it seemed, and he whispered roughly, "Are you sure you know what you're doing, Mary?"

"I know it's what I want," she whispered back. "When I saw you in the parking lot outside the store, I saw this. I saw you, and me. And I was terrified. But I'm not anymore. If anything, I'm scared that—"

"What, Mary? Tell me."

"I'm scared that you won't," she admitted, meeting his gaze squarely, determinedly, because truth was, she wasn't afraid to say it. She wasn't afraid to ask him to make love to her. Which was shocking, to say the least. Sexual confidence was a very new thing to her. Like, about two seconds old, that's how new. "Make love to me," she said simply.

He picked her up and took her toward the bed and it was exactly what she wanted him to do. Her body was on fire. She couldn't wait another second to make love with him.

It was crazy. Mind-boggling, in fact. Since when had she been the least bit impressed with sex? Making love with Danny had never left her anything but dissatisfied—when she could even talk him into participating. He'd let her know the lack was on her part, and the humiliation of that was enough to keep her from asking too often. Never in her wildest fantasies could she have seen herself jumping in the sack with such reckless abandon, with a virtual stranger, no less.

And he seemed just as eager. And he didn't feel like a stranger to her heart. Or to her body.

He set her down on the bed. She ripped the camo T-shirt over her head and fell back on the quilt-covered mattress, her breasts naked to him as she'd left her bra with her soaked clothes. He loomed over her, so strong, so powerful, and in his eyes she saw glorious, pounding need—for her! And yet she knew he would walk away this very moment if she told him she'd changed her mind.

As if! Breathless need blew through her as he tore off his own shirt and she reached out to him, pulling him down on top of her. He was already hard, and she wriggled against him, pressing that aching part of her into him, wanting to feel him.

His big, muscular body pinned her, hot and heavy, as he sought her lips again. She raked her fingers across his back, touching, exploring, desperate for every inch of him, as his tongue swept into her mouth. She drank him in. He tasted darkly erotic, his pure maleness as foreign to her as an uncharted sea, and she was so drunk with him, her head spun.

He slid away, just ever so slightly, so that he could slip his hand between them to touch the taut, aching tips of her bared breasts. She gasped at the contact and he released her mouth, looked down at her, his gaze soft and searing, as if waiting, and when she whispered, "Please," he dipped his head, slowly, so slowly, as her stomach jumped with anticipation, to take first one, then the other tight nub into his mouth. While she didn't so much as breathe, couldn't breathe, just fisted her hands in the quilt at her sides.

And moaned, oh yeah, that was her making that sound. Then he was kissing her everywhere, touching, licking, nipping, arousing her until all coherent thought fled her head. She didn't even know when he pulled the string that released the tie holding the drawstring pants at her waist, only knew his fingers skimming the very rim of her wanting, straining center. She pushed at the remains of her clothing, almost desperate, hands shaking, and he sat up, pulled the pants off. She wore no panties, having left them with the rest of her things along with her bra. He made quick work of his own clothes. He stood there for an endless moment, his hard body outlined by the dying kerosene glow, and her entire being quivered.

He came back to her, kissing her again, her lips, her eyelids, her chin, his mouth whispering molten fire every place they touched. And oh, she wanted him to touch her more and more and forever. She felt like she was going to explode already and she grabbed his hand, grabbed it and drew it down to the soft, damp fire between her legs. He teased his fingers inside her, shallow at first, flicking mercilessly, then deeper as hot ripples scorched her all over and her muscles clenched around him.

And she was sobbing, sobbing, at the shock waves of pure dizzying pleasure as he proceeded to drive her the rest of the way out of her mind.

While she was still shaking, he crawled up her body, pressing his most impressive heat against her throbbing core. He kissed her, softly, tenderly, then his fingers brushed her hair back and she opened her eyes to meet the stark loveliness of his.

Lovely. He had such lovely eyes for a man, long-lashed, dark, deep.

"Are you okay?" he whispered.

Her breath hitched as she struggled for the brain cells to form words.

"Yes," she whispered shakily. "Oh, my God. How did you do that?"

"That?"

"You know!"

"It's F.M.," he said solemnly.

"Are you going to tell me what F.M. means?"

"Freakin' magic."

She stared at him. He was magic, all right.

"Can you do it again?"

"Well, yes," he said, smiling in the shadows, smiling so sweetly, so funnily, as if she had said something quite hilarious. "All you have to do is ask."

She laughed out loud, almost choking on her still panting breaths.

"Asking," she managed to tell him.

And he did it. Right away. As if she had a genie at her command. She dug her nails into the hard muscles of his shoulder, hanging on for dear life as her mind blew apart.

She came to her senses, her body as limp as a rag doll, and realized with a sharp jolt of awareness that she was terribly, terribly selfish. She wanted to feel bad about it except she felt so damn good.

"Gideon?" she breathed against his ear where he lay against her, holding her as she still shuddered.

"Yes, Mary?" he whispered in the soaking darkness.

When had they lost all the light? She had no idea. All she knew was that he had the sexiest voice in the world and if he would just say her name over and over, she could almost explode again from listening to it.

"I want to ask you to do that again, but I feel selfish."

"I'll do it all you want."

Oh, God. He *was* a genie. Her genie. And he had a great big candy store of wishes all for her.

She reached for him, skimming her hand along his shoulder, down his arm, to his strong fingertips, to his naked and wow, so hard ass. Need pierced her, shockingly. How could she want him so constantly? She should have been alarmed, but she was too busy being thrilled and amazed.

"I want you inside me," she said.

"We don't have to do that if you don't want to, Mary."

"I want to!" she cried. How could he not know how much she wanted to? "I meant I want you to do that again, but I want you to do it inside me. Can you do that?"

Did she sound like an idiot? He sat up on his elbow. Her eyes, adjusting in the darkness, caught the gleam of his intense gaze.

"Mary, have you ever had an orgasm before tonight?"

She bit her lip, suddenly horribly embarrassed. She should not have made such a big deal of it. It was just that it *was* a big deal, to her.

"I just want you to feel good, too," she finally whispered.

"Making you feel good makes me feel good."

He meant that. She could tell. He really meant that.

"I just want to know—" Oh, God. Was she not done with fear? "I want to know if I can have an orgasm that way, too. Okay. So, no. I haven't ever had an orgasm before. At least not that I know about."

"I think you'd know," he said.

Oh yeah. She knew that *now.*

"I guess I thought before that maybe I had and I just hadn't noticed." That statement sounded laughable now.

But he didn't laugh. He reached his hand up and caressed her cheek.

"Mary—"

"I guess I knew I hadn't," she admitted. "I guess I thought—"

"What? You thought what?"

"I thought it was me." All the shame of years of unfulfilling sex rolled over her. And rolled away.

Gone. It hadn't been her. She'd certainly had no other experiences to judge. Danny had been her one and only lover.

"It wasn't you, Mary."

"Maybe you're just really good at it."

Now he laughed. "Oh, Mary, you are good. You are very good. No, great."

He was *so hot.* "You make me feel good. Great."

"That's the secret, Mary." He moved over, kissed her hotly, softly, whispering against her mouth, "that's all it is."

Something cracked inside her when he said that, something that brought a rush of fear. He could have no idea how much he'd touched her heart, and she didn't want to go there. This was about tonight, about healing, about a little slice of salvation for both of them. She couldn't let herself get it confused with anything else.

She reached between them, reached for him, that tangible part of him she *could* reach because she knew there was another, more intangible, piece of him that he'd never give her. She needed that consciousness-blinding freedom that he offered.

It was all she was going to get, and she'd be a fool not to be satisfied with the bounty of it.

"I want you," she whispered, wrapping her fingers around his hardness. He was huge. Wow.

And then he groaned out loud and he was kissing her, hungrily.

"Please, God," he rasped against her mouth when he let her go, "let me have a condom."

He slid off the bed and her heart beat hard, fearful—that he wouldn't. She hadn't even had the brain capacity to think of it. He moved in the dark. She could see him, shadow against shadow, going to the chair where he'd draped his things. She heard the rustle of him going through them, saw his shadow come back to the bed. His hands were soft on her, so achingly soft, and she'd never been so aware of her body and another's in her life.

"You sure?" he asked, and she managed to mumble yes before she couldn't speak anymore because he was stroking his thumb over her skin, along her ribs, down the curve of her waist, lower, and her legs, with a mind of their own, parted for him.

An almost unbearably sexy sound came out of him as he dipped his head down, to kiss her belly, then her hips, her thighs and there. Oh, there. He stroked his tongue unerringly exactly where she wanted him.

Just when she was about to die, he pulled up and she heard the rip of the foil packet, and then he was back, moving up her body, nudging that so amazing rock-hard part of him against her and she arched into him, wrapping her legs around him.

He pushed inside her with a low sound of pleasure that matched the one that escaped her mouth just before he captured it with his. And he held still there, thick and full and perfect, deep inside her as he kissed her.

How could this be so wonderful, so amazing, so *good?*

No, not good. Great.

Then he started to rock, and she was writhing, arching, absolutely begging in panting whispers against his mouth. And he seemed to know exactly how to give her what she needed. He slid a hand down the bare back of one thigh, pulling it up to his shoulder, then the other, allowing him deeper penetration. Then he reached between them to where they were joined and stroked right there, and she saw stars as he brought her to the very edge.

Then stopped, slowed, letting her come down off that near-explosion just before he brought her back up. Oh, God, the sweet torture of him. She wanted to kill him and keep him forever all at once.

She threw her head back, pleading, and he came down on his elbows, brushed the hair out of her face, kissed her dearly, and she was so glad it wasn't over because she never wanted this to end. He whispered her name and drew his head down, his mouth claiming the tips of her breasts and she fell apart all over the place.

He brought her back by rocking hard into her again, then faster, and she could not believe she was coming again. Aching, clawing need, and planet-spinning satisfaction, that's what he made her feel. And it felt so amazing.

Sensory overload of unbelievable proportions.

She opened her eyes, half expecting to see heaven, and did in a way—she saw his eyes. Locked with hers. She saw everything she felt in him, the pure need, the shocking dependency on one another for this perfect, perfect pleasure, and the edge she wanted to fall over again, with him. He pumped harder, faster, going rigid then pouring his release into her as she went off like a firecracker, dropping back to Earth in mindless, shaking flames.

The fast, heavy beat of his heart was the first thing

she became aware of. His heartbeat. His arms around her. The sweetly musky male scent of him. Her face was pressed against his shoulder, her lips against his neck.

He rolled to the side then, but didn't leave her, his arms staying tight across her belly. Intimate. Connected. A stranger no more.

He was her lover.

It was crazy, beyond crazy. And it was also amazing, fantastic, beautiful. It was a downright miracle.

Her heart still beat kind of wildly. She lay tucked up against his hard, sinewy body and she didn't want to move. She didn't want him to move. Her pulse gradually slowed. He spooned her even closer against him as he settled. Only the two of them existed. Here, there were no bad guys with guns. No pain, no loss. Just his deliciously warm arm wrapping her, his hand resting in sweet possession of her breasts as they fell into sleep together.

She woke to madness.

Chapter 10

Mary couldn't catch her breath. There were stairs, lots of stairs. She had to hurry. Molly was up there and she had to get her, and get her fast, because they were all in terrible danger. But the stairs wouldn't end. They went on and on. Molly was up there, turning her scissors this way and that, cutting out a yellow hat, a rain slicker, boots. She folded the flaps and put the outfit on her paper doll.

And Mary climbed and climbed the stairs.

It was hot outside and the sky was so blue. Molly wanted to go out to play, but she wasn't allowed. She heard the train and she put her doll down on the little red table and ran to the window.

She was high up here, so high. She could see the tops of trees.

Sugar maples, that's what her daddy said they were. She knew all the names of the trees, or at least most of them. She wished her daddy would come take her away. She could see the river and the pretty sailboats, and the big iron bridge. She was scared the bad man was going to come and say mean things again, and she didn't know why her grandfather would let that happen.

She missed her mommy even though she had trouble remembering what she looked like anymore. But she remembered what the bad man looked like.

The door. Mary finally reached the door. She gasped, panic shooting through her.

It was locked. She banged on it, hard. Banged and banged. Oh, God, she had to get in there and she had to hurry.

F.M. She needed Gideon's F.M.

She called to Molly, but Molly couldn't open the door. Why? She had to get to Molly. She was going to help Molly, and Molly was going to help her.

Below, she heard gunfire. Terror struck her heart. Gideon! Gideon was going to die! She had to hurry.

She found the breath to scream.

"Mary! I've got you. You're okay, I've got you."

She flailed against him, her eyes wide open and wild, unfocused. She was strong, fighting him with every ounce of her being, and she broke free, slammed him off her. He fell from the edge of the bed where they'd been wrapped tight in each other's arm. Fell on his ass, hard.

"Gideon!" she screamed, but she still wasn't looking at him. She bolted from the bed, tripped over him, and he caught her as she tumbled on him and fell back on the floor again, hard.

"Mary, I'm right here. I'm right here." Here, and nearly seeing stars because this time he'd hit his head.

"Gideon?" Her voice came out small, choked, and her glazed eyes focused on him finally, focused and held. She looked like she was in shock.

And she looked beautiful. Unbelievably, he felt himself go hard. He was in pain and he was hard for her. Totally outrageous. He should have had his fill of her last night. He never went back for seconds. Against his self-imposed rules since the divorce.

But, oh yeah, he wanted her. Even if afterward she knocked him on his ass again.

She scrambled off him, naked, gorgeous, her sweet, perfect breasts bobbing, her hair flying in abandon around her face. Her gaze locked on his very hard, sharp need and she blinked, twice, and lifted her tormented eyes to his face again.

"You were going to die. They were going to kill you."

The fiery desire washed cold.

"Who?"

"Them. Whoever. The bad guys!"

"You had a bad dream, Mary." If she started seeing him dead now, he didn't want to know about it. He was going after Molly. He didn't want to die, but there was no way he could keep on living if *she* died and there had been a chance in hell he could have saved her.

"You have to show me how you did that thing with the lock." Her breaths hitched as she half sobbed the request. Her eyes burned, hot and damp. "It wasn't a nightmare. It was not a nightmare!" she repeated, panic rising in her words.

"What thing with the lock?" She was losing him here.

"How you got us into the cabin. The F.M.!"

"What? Why?"

"I have to know how you did that! I'm going to need to know when we find Molly!"

"Mary, I already told you that you're not going with me."

"Yes, I am. I'm going to be there. I know where Molly is. I can help you find her."

"Where is she?"

"She's by a river. There are sailboats. Trees, sugar maples. An iron bridge. Train tracks. She can hear the train. She's somewhere very high, on a hill, maybe a house on a cliff. She's upstairs, way upstairs. I couldn't get up the stairs fast enough. The stairs just went on forever and I couldn't climb them fast enough."

He struggled to process her disjointed thoughts. "That sounds like a dream, Mary. You're trying to go up the stairs and you can't ever reach the top. That's like a dream."

"No, it's not!" She was shaking, her words coming out in panting gasps. "I saw Molly! I know the difference between a dream and what I see that's real. Sometimes I can't tell if parts of what I see are past or future, sometimes it's tangled up together, but I know that it's real. You have to believe me. I heard gunshots and I knew you were there, you were downstairs, and—"

And he was going to die. He didn't want to believe her. For the first time, he didn't want to believe in the very power he'd come to her to find.

But the stark ferocity of her eyes told him *she* believed it.

"I thought you could only see people and places you were familiar with."

"I'm familiar with you—and you're there. *I'm* there. I've opened my mind. I'm not scared of it, of this ability, anymore. I don't understand it, but I do know that when I let go of the fear, it's like it opens up to me. All I know is that I see Molly. And I hear gunshots and you're there. I know that they're going to kill you because I can't get to Molly quickly enough."

His pulse thumped. "Who are they? Where are we? What you just described could be any number of cities on the East Coast, Mary! Not to mention half the homes in Charleston. The judge's own house is on a cliff. You can see the river, train tracks. Maybe it's the past you're seeing, Molly at her grandfather's house."

It could also describe Venezia's estate in the hills overlooking the Kanawha River. Still, what Mary had described wasn't enough to go on. It wasn't anything more than a validation of where he suspected Molly could be. Still in Charleston. Under Venezia's control.

"I don't know," she said. "But I know I'm supposed to be there. I can find Molly!"

"No." He got up off the floor. "You're worried about me, I know that. You're scared. Maybe the whole thing is part nightmare, part sensory projection from the past, part fears. I appreciate that you're scared for me. It's touching even. But that doesn't mean you can help me."

She seemed to suddenly realize she was nude. She spun, looked for her clothes. The camo T-shirt and pants were tossed wildly on the floor. She dived for them, pulled them on quickly.

Dressed, face flushed, she planted her hands on her hips and looked like she was trying really hard to ignore the fact that he wasn't worried about his own bare-assed state.

She was also ignoring what he'd had to say.

"You need to show me how to do that thing with the lock so I can get to Molly. I'm going to need to know. You can teach me about guns now, too."

"No."

"You told me you'd teach me to shoot sometime."

"There's going to be all kinds of law enforcement looking for me, and for you, all over these hills today, Mary," he pointed out. "They probably think I kidnapped you. We're not directing them to us by firing off any rounds."

She couldn't argue with that, but she could still argue.

"I need to know how to get through a locked door." She froze, stumbled back on what he'd said. "How are we going to get out of here?"

"I have a plan."

Her face took on an exasperated expression. "I know you have a plan. You always have a plan. What is it?"

"You're not coming with me, Mary. I'm going to find some place for you to hide out, and then I'm going on without you."

Her mouth set in a pissy line. "I know that I am going with you because I saw it, so this is a pointless discussion."

"Yeah, well, you say I'm going to get shot if you aren't there and can't get through the door to Molly, so apparently you think you can change the future. I can change it, too. You're not coming with me."

He was really starting to wish he hadn't talked her into believing in herself, but just looking at her—gorgeous, hot-eyed and confident… He couldn't regret a thing despite his frustration. She was not the same scared, haunted woman he'd met yesterday.

But no way was he putting her in any more danger. He wanted her *out* of danger. Including the danger of him and what they'd done last night and couldn't repeat.

He wanted to slide his arms around her, put his hands in her hair, kiss her neck and fall together onto the bed and make love to her so slowly. And he couldn't do that. Never again. And that was just one more reason he needed to find a safe place to stash her until this whole thing blew over, and he needed to find it as soon as possible.

The gaze he squared on her was steady and as hard as he could make it.

"Now get your things. We're getting out of here."

Gideon put on his clothes, and Mary didn't know if she was relieved or sorry. He moved like a sleek tiger, all fluid motion, easy grace, unwavering determination to ignore her. Her genie was back in his bottle.

Just thinking about last night nearly made her head spin. She'd probably follow him to the ends of the Earth just for another taste of that heaven, and if anything scared her now, it was that. Meanwhile, he was quite clearly all done with her.

Whether that was because he'd had his fill of her and didn't want her anymore, or because he was so focused on his mission, she wasn't sure. She knew they were going to make love again, and she wasn't sure of how she knew that, either.

Maybe it was just wishful thinking. She had no control of this psychic ability she had just barely accepted, and she needed to focus, too, on sticking with Gideon and saving Molly.

He sat down at the kitchen table and studied a map he'd gotten from somewhere. Morning light yawned in, misty and pale, through the small window over the sink.

You think you can change the future.

Could she? Or could she only see things as they would absolutely happen? She had no idea.

"How are we getting out of here?" she repeated her question, coming up behind him to look over his shoulder at the crinkled, faded map spread out before him.

"Oil roads. Hunters use them. I found this map in the chest. Some of them are probably still in use and kept cleared by gas and oil companies doing work out here." Highlighted lines crisscrossed the old paper. "I'm guessing these are some of the trails whoever owns this cabin has used. See." He pointed, drew his finger along a line, connected to another, then another. "We can get out of the county this way. And no one the wiser. Or so we hope."

She leaned to follow the line he drew, and the musky-male scent of him came to her. She had to tell herself not to touch him and she wanted to, badly. She moved back as he pushed his chair from the table. He folded the map and got his things.

"Ready?" he asked.

The intensity of his eyes burned a hole through her. He looked starkly handsome standing there and she didn't want to leave the cabin. Out there, the world was so brutal and dangerous. They might not even make it out of Haven.

She'd seen them finding Molly, though. She had to keep believing in a power she didn't understand or she'd never bring herself to walk out that door.

She took a deep breath. "Ready as I'll ever be."

Gold shimmers dazzled the tops of the trees as they stepped outside. She walked onto the porch. She could hear birds cooing in the woods, the rustle of leaves swaying in the light wind.

It was still chilly from the overnight dip in temperature, but the sky was robin's egg–blue. It was going to be a nice day.

She turned to watch him shut the door as he came out. She didn't move to leave the porch.

"Show me how you opened that lock last night," she said again.

"Planning on taking up a life of crime, Mary?"

Smart-ass. He knew what she was after.

"Yes. Exactly." When he looked as if he was going to remind her, once more, that she was *not* going with him to find Molly, she cut him off. "We don't have all day, so just show me how to do it and then we can argue about the rest of it in the car."

"Lock picking is a skill that requires practice. There are a lot of different lock designs and variations. You're not going to learn it in five minutes."

"Try me. Explain the basic concept." She knew the lock she had to pick was like this one.

"Fine." He whipped out his pocketknife and extended a long, thin piece of metal with a curve at the tip. "You understand how locks work, Mary?"

"They keep people out."

At least the look he gave her was amused, not impatient.

"A lock is like a puzzle," he said. "There's a series of pins of different lengths, divided up in pairs. Each pair sits in a shaft with springs holding them in position. When you put in the right key, all the pins are pushed up and you can open the door. To open it without a key, you've got to insert the pick and lift up each pin pair to the right position. You can hear a click as they fall on the ledge of the shaft."

He demonstrated.

"Hear that?" he said softly.

"No."

He lifted up the next set of pins. "Now?"

Barely. She'd barely heard something. "How did you do it so fast?" It hadn't taken him any time at all to break into the cabin the night before.

"Practice. It's a difficult skill to master, Mary.

You can't expect to learn it in the next couple of minutes and use that skill to save Molly. Or me. To pick a lock successfully, you've got to hone your sense of touch, feel the very slight forces of the moving pins, know the sounds and understand the mechanisms so well that you are able to visualize the pieces inside the lock as if you could see them." He pulled the pick out. "Let's go."

"Wait." She put her hand over his, took the pick back. "Let me try again."

Believe in herself, that was the key. Open her mind. No fear.

She slid the pick into the lock and saw the pins, lifting the first pair up in its housing. The sound of the upper pin falling onto the ledge of the shaft clicked in the cool, quiet morning. She saw the next one, and the next one, and she felt the beat of her pulse, excitement bursting inside her even as she concentrated so hard, she almost forgot he was standing there. She saw the pins, each pair, where they were, where she had to apply pressure, exactly. She could *see* them.

And she turned the knob, opened the cabin door.

Her gaze swung, shocked, to Gideon. She had just about taken her own breath away and she couldn't speak for a full beat.

"I saw inside the lock," she said finally. "Oh, my God."

She dropped the tool set. It clacked on the wooden

floor of the porch. Her heart beat so hard, she thought it might bang right out of her chest.

What else could she do with this power of sensory projection? She wanted, and was a little scared, to find out.

The expression on Gideon's face was dark and completely impenetrable to her.

"Get in the car, Mary." His voice was low, angry.

Oh, he didn't like this at all. Not one bit.

"Did you see what I can do?" she asked.

"Get in the car," he repeated.

He bent, picked up the tool set, shut the door and turned away from her, took the steps off the cabin porch, strode toward the Impala and banged inside it. The sound of the engine turning over kicked through the dewy-soft morning.

She followed him to the car, a strange sense of calm settling over her. He was going to need her. And he didn't have the market cornered on determination.

Chapter 11

"And we're going to make love again, too," she said after she sat down in the car. "But not right now. Later."

Gideon didn't know whether to laugh or strangle her or just look forward to it. He had created a monster.

"I'm driving," he said. "I don't generally make love while operating a moving vehicle."

He sliced a glance at her as the Impala rolled down the overgrown drive to the road. She watched him with a curious mixture of steel-magnolia determination and endearing embarrassment at what had popped out of her mouth. This new power she'd accepted in herself had emboldened her to say and do things he didn't think she would have before and she wasn't completely comfortable with it. But that determination was carrying her forward anyway. As much as she'd fretted that his emotions might cause him to take risks he shouldn't, he was worried this new determination of hers was going to cause her the same problem.

Then it struck him that he hadn't even argued the point that they would make love again. And he sure as hell hoped that wasn't an example of emotion messing with his risk assessment.

Mary had him so turned upside down, he didn't know what he was doing, that was all.

The way to the oil track he planned to follow wasn't far. His grip on the wheel tightened as he turned out onto the narrow road. The track led up to the right about a quarter mile down and he shifted into lower gear to make it up the rutted dirt and rock trail. He'd set the map on the dash and Mary took it down, opened it up and started navigating.

She shouldn't look so daisy-fresh and pretty in the same camo T-shirt and drawstring pants she'd worn the night before, but she did. She wore no makeup other than some lip gloss she'd put on at some point. Lip gloss that smelled really good, like some kind of cookie, and he wondered if it was that sort of gloss that tasted just as delicious....

Focus. He was in desperate need of focus.

"So what's our plan for the day?" she asked, putting the map in her lap.

The oil track they were on now went several miles before the next turnoff. It showed evidence of usage in the near past, deep tire ruts that looked fairly fresh. The overhanging woods closed in around them, underbrush scraping along the sides of the car. Both the rear and front passenger windows were shot out, but otherwise they were good to go as long as they didn't get lost and run out of gas before they made it back to a real road and a gas station. The oil tracks would take them out across the county line in a place no one would be expecting them to be, so hopefully they'd avoid any road blocks that might have been set up. He had no idea what was going on in the world.

He flicked on the radio, tuned in to a local news station.

"We're going to get out of here and find some place to pick up some things," he said. "Gas for starters. Clothes, food. Then I'm going to find a safe place to leave you."

He'd been turning ideas over in his head. He had to get back to Charleston, but heading for a hotel in the heart of the city didn't sound like a good idea. Too much exposure to the public.

He needed to find some out-of-the-way place, outside the city. Outside Haven. A place where they wouldn't ask too many questions.

His main trouble would be convincing Mary to stay put, but she was distracted by the next story on the radio before she could start arguing with him again.

"Teams of county sheriff's detectives fanned out over a wide area surrounding Haven searching for clues in the suspected abduction last night of a thirty-two-year-old Haven woman."

"Oh, my God, that's me." She reached for the radio knob at the same time as he did. He put his hand back on the wheel, shocked by the reaction just touching her wrought inside him.

Like taking one sip of water when you were dying of thirst. He wanted to touch her all over. Dammit.

"Officials brought out search dogs and helicopters this morning. The incident began with a shooting yesterday evening at a grocery store parking lot in Haven. A suspect vehicle involved in the shooting was burned in an explosion at the scene, but witnesses said the occupant of the car fled the scene on foot. A second suspect fled in a late-model black Impala with a woman identified as Haven resident Marysia O'Hurley.

"Sheriff's deputy Steve Theiss said he did not believe the woman, missing since last night, left the scene of her own free will and they are treating the disappearance as a kidnapping. No injuries were reported from the explosion, which is believed to have been caused by the first suspect's vehicle impacting a propane tank. The search for O'Hurley and the two suspects in the shooting forced the closure of highways in and out of the county overnight and officials continue searching today.

"O'Hurley is described as a white female with brown hair and blue eyes. She is five feet six inches tall and weighs about one hundred and twenty-five pounds. Investigators are searching for a black Impala, possible year model two thousand four or two thousand five."

A commercial jingle followed the end of the story. Mary turned the volume back down.

"Oh, God, people must be so worried about me." She sounded horrified. "At least I know everyone was okay at the store."

"There's nothing you can do right now, Mary," Gideon told her. He felt her pain, but she had to know she couldn't contact anyone back in Haven. "You don't want to put any of your friends in danger."

"No." She was quiet a beat. "They didn't say anything about you. I mean, your name, or anything about the U.S. Marshals. That's good, right?"

"They said something about helicopters," Gideon said. That wasn't good at all. Taking these old oil tracks out of the county wouldn't help them if a chopper spotted them overhead, but at this point the best they could do was continue on. There was plenty of cover if he heard them in time.

He wasn't surprised his name hadn't been released to the media, or any information about the incident at headquarters last night. Tucker was going to play this his way, and for now, that worked for Gideon, too.

"Keep your ears peeled," he said.

"Okay."

She sounded scared again.

"This will be over soon," he told her. One way or the other.

Neither one of them spoke as he negotiated the turnoff to another oil track. The path, such as it was, only got worse. It was another thirty minutes before they came down a ridge to a blacktop road. If they were where he thought they were, they were out of Haven, out of the county, and they shouldn't hit any roadblocks.

The interstate shouldn't be too far away, another five miles, but he wasn't going that way, not now. He couldn't risk the exposure.

He went in the opposite direction, finding the two-lane main highway into a small town where he stopped for gas at old-fashioned, rusted pumps in front of a small one-story building called Hildreth's Country Store. The name of the town posted on the store's sign was Lincoln's Mill. They'd come out on the other side of the county line, as he'd expected.

"Go on inside," he told Mary. "I'll be right in. Pick up anything you need."

She gave him a look that pulled somehow at his chest. She was cooperating, but he knew she was making her own plans. And she was worried about him, that's what that look in her eyes told him. He wasn't used to having anyone worry about him, not for a long time, and it was a strange, achy feeling.

"How long until you try to get rid of me?" she asked.

"As soon as possible."

"I'm not a baby," she said. "I don't need to be dropped off at day care. You've made your choices about this mission that isn't assigned to you. You have no right to interfere with what are *my* choices to make."

She tipped her chin, holding his gaze with resolute steadiness. It was unbelievable to him how pretty she looked, how sweet and strong.

Hell, he had it bad for her, that was all there was to it.

"I'm real proud of you, Mary," he added, the praise popping out of his mouth without thought. "I know this has been hard. And I know what I'm going to ask you to do next seems hard to you, too, but it's the right thing to do. I want you to be safe, and I need you to help me do that."

He needed to be pushing her away and he realized instantly that his words had been a mistake. Her gaze softened, tearing at the already crumbling walls of his heart.

"I like you, too," she said, and got out of the car, slamming the door behind her, leaving him without a word to say.

Well. She didn't know what to make of him.

Mary thought about Gideon's words, the unexpected praise that had her melting into a mushy puddle. He seemed so detached, almost defiantly so, and yet at the same time he was so kind to her, and so protective. Was she just part of his job or did he have a personal stake with her, too, as he had with Molly?

It was getting real personal for her.

Was she cruising for a bruising? He was like some kind of pulse-pounding cliffhanger and she kept wanting to turn the page. But there was a little bit, okay a lot, of fear there. And as with the power of her sensory projection, she'd have to shake that fear, risk everything, to figure out the truth.

So that made the real question, how bad did she want that truth?

Wow. She was having more dramatic lightning strikes of clarity than she was sure she could handle in a twenty-four-hour period.

The little store inside the gas station was cute, much smaller than the Foodway in Haven, but it still offered a variety of basic groceries and other goods. The store smelled like grease and meat and quite honestly it smelled like heaven. She was starving. There was a small deli counter in the back with a round-the-clock menu.

She went to the counter to read the menu, saw Gideon through the glass in the store window, striding across the pavement toward the building. He looked out of place, but maybe that was just her. She couldn't look at him without seeing curling flames behind him on the action movie poster.

The bell on the door jingled as he entered and zeroed in on her.

"Got everything you need?" he asked.

"I don't need anything but food right now. I'm hungry."

"We're in a hurry."

"I'm hungry," she repeated. "I see myself eating a big cheeseburger."

Okay, she'd made him laugh.

"I'm going to start getting suspicious about this whole thing," he said.

"I see you eating a big cheeseburger, too," she said. "How's that?"

"I guess I can deal with that."

She turned to lean back against the counter while they waited. There was a TV over the register up front and the national morning news and talk show broke for the local station. In Lincoln's Mill, as in Haven and several surrounding counties, that meant Charleston.

"Federal judge Alcee Reinhold resigned this morning in a move that surprised friends and foes alike. The judge cited personal reasons for the decision. The judge's daughter passed away two years ago, and a source close to the judge reported that Reinhold plans to spend more time with his family.

"Reinhold had once been considered on the short list for a Supreme Court nomination before taking a top position at the controversial technology think tank, MicroCorp. He returned to the federal bench six years ago and is being called a hero for his record of strong rulings despite recent flip-flopping that drew criticism from many within the law enforcement community."

Mary glanced at Gideon. The brooding intensity of his expression was hard to read.

Then it hit her.

"Why hasn't there been anything on the news about Molly?"

He turned back to her, taking his attention from the television.

"The story was not released to the media."

"Will this help Molly? That he's resigned now?" Something fluttered at the edges of her mind. The judge's photo flashed on the television screen she could still see over Gideon's shoulder as the news announcer detailed the judge's history on the bench.

"That would be nice," Gideon said quietly. "But kidnappers don't usually release their victims alive. That's why I've got to convince Venezia it's in his best interest to do so this time."

There was a photograph of another man on the screen now. The caption underneath read Nicholas Venezia. The broadcaster finished up her story with a reference to the federal government's long probe into the Pittsburgh mafia's resurgence in West Virginia under Venezia.

The fluttering at the edges of her mind sharpened into a hot streak, almost painful and she could hear

Venezia speak. She stared at his picture in the small box to the left of the news anchor on the screen.

"Get that fucking judge back on the bench!"

Venezia was screaming. Screaming.

She blinked, stared at the screen. Venezia's picture was gone and some guy was discussing the five-day forecast. Clear today. Storms moving in toward evening, then sunny the rest of the week. Highs in the eighties.

"Hey."

She felt weirdly numb and tingly all at once. She realized Gideon wasn't standing in front of her anymore. She turned around, following his voice. He stood behind her, holding a paper deli bag. Their cheeseburgers were ready.

"Do you want to get something to drink?" he asked.

"Venezia doesn't want the judge off the bench," she said. Breathless. She felt like her lungs were choked. "He wants him on."

Gideon stared at her. "What?"

"He wants him *on!*"

He took her arm. "That doesn't make sense, Mary." He almost shook her. She realized she was talking too loudly and that she was close to having a panic attack and she didn't know why.

She was scared out of her mind. Scared for Molly. Something was wrong.

"We have to get out of here," Gideon said.

She blinked, followed his sharp gaze. Outside, a local sheriff's car had pulled up and a deputy was walking around the back of the Impala.

Their luck had just run out.

Chapter 12

Gideon moved fast. He grabbed two bottles of water and handed the deli clerk a handful of bills. "This is for the gas, too," he said.

"You'll have to take that to the other register. I can't take that here."

"Yes, you can."

He was done with the deli clerk and he was about to take a huge risk. He turned.

"Walk away from me. Look around the store. Shop. Don't buy anything. When I get in the car, come outside. Don't let that deputy see your face."

Adrenaline throbbed hard through his veins. He forced his feet to slow to a nice, casual pace as he left the building.

The sheriff's deputy stood beside his car, looked up at him.

"Is this your vehicle?" the officer asked as he reached him.

"Yes, sir."

"Got some damage here." He was inspecting the shot-out windows. The glass had splintered out enough that it wasn't obvious the damage came from bullets.

"Parked under the wrong tree last night in that storm."

"I'd like to see some identification."

Gideon reached into his pocket, brought out his driver's license, then flipped open his U.S. Marshal credentials.

"I apologize," the deputy said, his tone shifting to deferential. "They're hunting a suspect driving a late-model black Impala in the next county. Just doing my duty here."

"I understand. I'm on vacation, getting a little R & R at a cabin out here, but I heard about that case. Missing woman, possible kidnap victim."

"That's the one. Have a good day. Was just stopping here for some sausage biscuits. They sure make 'em good here."

"Sure do." Gideon held up the bag. "Got something from the counter myself."

The deputy entered the store. Through the window, he could see the officer walk straight back to the deli counter. Mary had been loitering between the aisles.

He opened the car and she made a beeline for the door of the store, the bell jingling as she came out. She got in the car and he pulled away from the gas pumps.

Slow, nonchalant. They hit the first curve on the highway and he floored it.

After about five minutes, she spoke.

"That freaked me out," she said.

"It was a risk," he told her. His grip on the steering wheel was only just starting to relax. As he'd suspected, local law enforcement wasn't completely clued in. Tucker would have made sure of that.

But if he'd tried to tell that deputy his story…

The first thing he'd have done would be contact the Marshals and then Gideon would be fried. He needed proof. He needed Venezia.

"The farther we get from Haven, the safer we'll be," he said.

A missing woman was big news in and around Haven, but in the city, there was a lot more going on.

"That's not what I meant."

He shot Mary a glance. Her eyes were wide, haunted. In the heat of the moment, he'd almost forgotten what she'd said back at the deli counter.

"What you said about Venezia—"

"He wants Judge Reinhold on the bench, not off," she repeated.

"That doesn't make sense."

"I know. Something's wrong. And I'm scared. I'm scared about Molly. If Venezia wants the judge on the bench, why would he be involved in kidnapping Molly and threatening the judge?"

"We know Venezia's involved. We know Tucker's involved. And we know what they have to want out of Reinhold."

That much was crystal clear.

"But Venezia wants the judge on the bench," she said again. "You have to believe me!"

His grip on the wheel tightened. He didn't know what to believe. What Mary was saying now didn't fit. Could this be one of those times she was wrong?

"All I know is that Venezia has the answers," he said. "And I'm going to get them."

He had a deal and it was a deal Venezia couldn't turn down.

"What if he lies to you? You need me there. You need me to tell you what's true. I'll know if Venezia's lying. I know you want to nail Tucker if he was involved in that bombing. But I know you want even more to save Molly. Venezia can save himself without turning over Molly, don't you see that? What if there's no proof he was behind Molly's kidnapping?"

"I'm not risking your life, Mary."

"I don't give a rat's ass what you want to risk!" she shouted at him. "You don't get to decide for me! You don't run the world and you sure as hell don't run me!"

Gideon swore and gravel crunched as he yanked the wheel and pulled the car to the side of the road. Mary braced herself against the dash at the sharp stop.

His hot, angry gaze bored into her.

"I'll be damned if I'm going to let you get killed, Mary."

"Let me? *Let* me?" she repeated. "Who put you in charge of me? Oh, wait a minute, I forgot, you're in charge of everything!"

"I have a responsibility to protect you. I made an oath—"

"An oath to whom? The Marshals? Don't give me that crap." She knew he took his role in law enforcement seriously, but she also knew that this wasn't about the law. "Why did you come for me last night?"

He stared at her. "I needed your help. Now I need to keep you safe."

"Keep me safe? Or keep yourself safe?"

"Mary—"

"I'm not done helping you," she said. "I know things, I see things. I can help you. What are you really afraid of, Gideon? Are you afraid we got too close last night, that if we spend more time together, we'll get even closer?"

Sparks fired in his eyes. She could almost hear his heart pounding. Oh yeah, he was scared of something. And right now, she wasn't.

"I don't want to be responsible for anyone else getting hurt!" he exploded.

"Anyone *else?*"

Silence, taut, crushed down inside the car. There

was nothing but the low hum of the Impala's motor for a long moment.

Gideon fixed his gaze on the road ahead. "We're going to an out-of-the-way motel I know about, and I'm leaving you there."

They'd be on their way right now, she knew, if he wasn't so angry, he couldn't drive. She wasn't planning to let up, either.

"Tell me what happened to Lizzie."

"We're not talking about Lizzie."

She was treading on fragile ground. She didn't want to touch Gideon's pain. It was damn clear he didn't want to go there, and truthfully she had no right to go there if he didn't want to.

But if she didn't...

It was his shield, that pain. It was where the action hero stopped and the real man began.

And if she didn't get to the real man, he might end up a *dead* man. That truth she hadn't been sure she was brave enough to uncover...

It was there, too.

She was brave enough. She had to be.

Deep breath.

"Did you think you were responsible for Lizzie's death? Did you think your job made her a target?"

His gaze snapped back to her.

"They never found her killer, did they?" She saw it all through his tortured eyes. "They found her body, but they never found who murdered her. You were with the State Police then. Your wife thought somebody you'd put away had done it, gotten out of prison and come after your family. You thought so, too, didn't you? But you could never prove it, never figure out who—"

"Yes, you know it all, Mary," he ground out, his voice so low and harsh, it took her breath away. "She divorced me. She didn't want anything to do with me after that. She blamed me for Lizzie's death. And yeah, I blamed myself, too. You think I want anybody close to me after that?"

His voice rose sharply. "But you must know that, too, so why the hell are you asking me?"

She swallowed hard, the pain in the car almost choking her. Horrible images swamped her. She could see Gideon on the side of a road somewhere, a tiny body being lifted out of a ditch, so badly decomposed. She could feel his agony, his rage.

His guilt. Most of all, his guilt.

"You weren't responsible for what happened to Lizzie. You weren't responsible for what happened to Molly, either. And you aren't responsible for whatever happens to me. There are terrible people in the world. They do terrible things. You're one of the good guys. Pushing everyone away from you, never letting anyone close, doesn't punish them. It only punishes you."

His next words were harsh and fast. "Who says I want to be close to you, Mary?"

Her own pain flared inside her now. Maybe she hadn't been brave enough for the truth, after all.

She looked straight ahead at the road, her tears causing the blacktop to blur.

"Mary—"

She felt his hand on her shoulder. She ignored it. "We don't have time to sit here. I'm sorry I brought up such a painful subject. I'm very sorry about your daughter and your marriage."

"I don't want to hurt you."

Her throat burned raw. "Too late."

It was her own fault. She couldn't blame him. She'd pushed, way past his limits, and she deserved whatever she got out of it. Believing that didn't make the shock and hurt any less, though.

"Mary—"

"Would you just drive?" She slammed her gaze to his for a tortured beat. "And just so you know, I'm going with you to find Molly. I'm seeing this through to the end unless you intend to tie me up and knock me out. I'm done talking about it, that's all. I get it, okay? I got a little bit stupid, thinking…."

She let her words trail away, glanced back at the road. Nope, not going there. She had her limits, too. And she was as far past hers as he was his.

"You really can't stop me, you know?" she pointed out. "You can leave me wherever the hell you want to and I can get a car and come after you. If you're so worried about protecting me, you might as well take me with you. But whatever. Do what you want, macho man. I'll do what I want."

There was another strained beat. His touch left her shoulder.

He jerked the car back into motion and they hit the road again. Yeah, he was about as happy as she was right now. He could blow off her feelings, but he couldn't blow *her* off. He was stuck with her, at least when it came to saving Molly.

And after that—

Nothing.

There was no *after that,* not when it came to her and Gideon.

Her entire body trembled with the stew of emotions she'd let so near the surface. An idiot, that's what she was. Wearing her heart on her sleeve. And wasn't that just her life story?

She wrapped her arms tight around herself. Thick woods whipped by as the car flew along the winding highway north. She had no idea what he was thinking and she didn't want to know.

Gideon steeled himself against the pain he knew he'd caused Mary. She was killing him. He'd told her he didn't want to hurt her and he'd meant it, but he couldn't say more. He'd said too much already.

Done too much already.

And yet he still couldn't regret making love to her.

The hell of it all was that he still wished he could do it again.

Sooner or later, she'd get it, for real. He didn't have more to give her than what he'd already given. She'd grown, changed, just in the short time he'd known her, and if he'd had anything to do with it, then he was glad. But his heart had shut down for business a long time ago now and he wasn't opening it back up. He didn't *want* to open it back up.

Something inside him twisted slowly and deeply, but he ignored it. It would go away.

The sky was crystal clear. He kept them off the interstate as they took a circuitous path on country roads. He found a discount department store on the outskirts of Charleston. They were on the seedier side of the city, but in their situation, it was the safer side.

People didn't talk to police here. Law enforcement was an enemy, not a friend, in this neighborhood. He didn't need any busybodies or do-gooders today.

Mary had barely spoken a word, but she hadn't needed to. She'd nailed the fatal flaw in his plan to get rid of her. He wanted to be angry with her for trapping him into taking her with him, but he couldn't help being proud of her, too.

She had courage, damn her. All he wanted to do was protect her, but she didn't want his protection. She was strong. Amazing, actually. She should be running for the hills, more than willing to hide out, but she wouldn't do it.

And as long as she was in this thing, whether he liked it or not, they were in it together because no way was he letting her go it alone. That was a risk he couldn't take.

He looked at her as he pulled into a parking spot in the discount store lot. Her profile was fragile in the sunshine streaking bright outside the car.

Mary turned and her eyes caught his. The memory of how soft and perfect she'd felt in his arms last night crept unbidden into his mind. He felt a possessiveness toward her he had no right to feel, a desire and longing that could only go unsatisfied.

"We'll find some place to stop and get cleaned up," he said. "So pick up some clothes, whatever you need." He was planning to pick up his insurance—video camera and tapes.

"And then we find Venezia?"

"If I can't talk you out of it."

"Right back at you," she said.

"You're pretty stubborn."

"It's a character flaw."

"It's not your character I'm worried about."

"You don't need to worry about me." There was a bitter light in her eyes.

"You don't seem to be giving me any choice about that."

A slow beat slid between them.

"Everyone has choices, Gideon," she said quietly. "People just make the wrong ones sometimes."

Chapter 13

Mary pushed out of the car and strode across the parking lot toward the bank of automatic sliding doors at the front of the store without waiting for Gideon. Maybe it was the thought of a hot shower and clean clothes driving her. Or probably the tears, stupid tears, that had stung her eyes when she'd had the nerve to throw that last comment at him.

She'd spent the better part of the past hour ignoring him and trying to talk herself into believing she didn't care if he had no feelings for her, or more likely, wasn't capable of having feelings for her.

Boy, could she pick them. First Danny, a decent enough guy if you didn't mind being emotionally and sexually neglected. Now Gideon Brand, who—wow, certainly knew how to treat a woman right in bed, but when it came to emotion… He was no better than Danny.

Maybe she had a thing for men who didn't want her. Some kind of masochistic desire to be thwarted.

She was going to have a rough life if she kept that up. Despite her best intentions, she had developed feelings for Gideon Brand, a mistake if she'd ever heard of one.

Gideon caught up with her inside the store. He looked hard and mysterious, as usual. She didn't have the slightest idea how they were going to find Venezia.

"What kind of clothes am I shopping for?" she asked coolly. That was it, cool. Get her act together. And it *was* an act.

"Something nice," he said. "We're going to hit a few restaurants and clubs, locations Venezia is known to frequent."

Nice. Hmm. This was hardly a fine retail outlet, but she would have to make do.

"What if we don't find him? What's the backup plan?"

His gaze bored into her. What was she saying? Like he needed a backup plan. He could probably conjure up Venezia at one of those locations by sheer force of his will.

The thought of confronting the crime boss with Gideon's deal left her so nervous, her stomach felt sick. Something was very wrong with their theory, she just didn't know what.

"Let's split up." He nodded toward the women's department. The men's department was on the other side. "I'll meet you at the register. Pick up anything else you need while you're at it."

At least he wasn't trying to get rid of her anymore, so she supposed she should be grateful for small favors even if he was, obviously, ignoring the emotionally-charged comment she'd tossed at him before leaving the car. He was all business now. It was as if the night before had never happened.

He could turn on and off as if he had a switch. Must be nice.

She focused on the task at hand, began sorting through racks of cheap clothing. Putting an outfit together that was dressy yet not tacky was a challenge. She eventually settled for a sleeveless white blouse with tiny pearl buttons and a pair of black pants. She spent way too much time in shoes before she found the perfect pair of slingback gold sandals in her size, then remembered undergarments and headed back to the intimates department but got sidetracked by jewelry. Everything was so inexpensive! She couldn't believe the cute bracelets for a dollar each. She should get into the city more often. At least it was a good distraction from her thoughts. She forced herself to settle for just a couple of pieces then went on to Intimates.

Her arms were getting full by the time she'd made her way across the store to pick up a few basic toiletries. She came around an aisle and bumped straight into Gideon, managing to drop her whole pile.

She stooped to pick up the clothing, toothpaste, toothbrush, shoes and other items she'd scattered at his feet.

Including the skimpy black panties she hadn't been able to resist.

Which he started to pick up as he helped her gather her things then carefully did *not*. She reached for the panties, pulled them into her arms and took the other items he handed her.

Granny panties, that's what she should have gone for. Now he probably thought she had ideas about those hot black ones. They looked like panties with a plan.

"Done shopping?" he asked, straightening. He held his hand out to help her up.

She ignored him, got up on her own. "Think so." Darting a look at him, she saw a flicker of something in his eyes. She was afraid it was pity.

He'd made it clear that whatever delusions she had about the two of them, it wasn't happening. She didn't want to get pathetic here.

"I happen to like sexy underwear," she said stiffly. "Don't get the wrong idea."

"I'm not going to attack you, Mary."

Dammit. She cast him a glowering look while he stood there all cool and in control and oozing his F.M. that made her knees, and other parts, tremble.

"Let's just go." She gave him her back and strode off toward the registers.

Paid, they got in the car and headed down a maze of side streets until they parked in front of a motel.

"Sorry about the not-so-five-star accommodations," he said. "The place is clean and safe."

She looked at the seedy building. Siding with peeling paint, cracked sidewalks, overgrown landscaping. The sign by the road leaned slightly to the left. It boasted cable TV and high-speed Internet.

"If it has a shower, it'll do," she said.

Gideon checked in at the office while she waited in the car. He pulled around to the back where he parked in front of one in a row of faded red doors. He unlocked the room with the key—the motel was so old, it actually had real room keys—flipping on the light switch as he held the door open for her. The switch activated a lamp on a dresser.

"Don't panic," he said. "We're not spending the night."

They'd spent last night in the same bed, much less the same room, so it was pitiful that it was all so awkward now. Her fault, she reminded herself. She was the one who'd gone and gotten emotional.

Nobody had made any promises last night. They'd made love. They'd given each other something they needed in the moment. It was her problem if that didn't feel like enough now.

"I'm not worried about it," she said coolly as she entered past him. "You don't need to tell me ten times over that you don't want me."

He was right about the place being clean, if somewhat shabby. There was one king-size bed made up with a thin bedspread in a faded orange-and-blue-checked pattern. Drapes hid the view of the parking lot outside. Mary dropped her bag on a table flanked by two upholstered chairs and moved the drapes slightly. The motel was on a slight rise and there was a view of the city across the river.

Between tall buildings, she glimpsed the bright gold of the Capitol dome.

"I never said I didn't want you, Mary."

She turned back, caught his hard, dark gaze. He'd shut the door. The light on the dresser left the main part of the room in shadows. Shadows that yawned between them like a giant gulf. He held two bags, one with the clothes he'd purchased, another with video accessories, tapes. A box containing a camera was on the floor where he'd pushed it through the door with his foot after setting it down to unlock the room.

"Semantics," she said briefly. She felt a choking lump in her throat.

She'd had enough of this conversation already. She picked up the TV remote and turned on the cable. Her favorite daytime small claims court show was on. She loved reality judge shows. Especially this one, with the ferocious lady judge who kicked ass and took names. She turned the volume up, a clear message.

She picked her now-cold cheeseburger out of the bag and ate it while Gideon messed around with the video equipment and she pretended he didn't exist. Pretended he didn't exist except for the part where she was thinking about him constantly and watching him out of the corner of her eye.

"I'm going to take a shower now," she told him when she'd finished. Like he cared. He was absorbed in the equipment.

She took her bag and headed for the other room.

The bathroom was all gleaming white tile and stainless steel fixtures. Apparently recently updated. Nice, very nice. From an outhouse in the wild woods to modern convenience.

She wouldn't mind one teeny bit if she could live that night in the cabin all over again. And she was actually crying, but he couldn't see her, so it didn't matter. She could cry all she wanted.

Then she realized it *did* matter. She didn't want to be weak anymore. She didn't want to cry. She wanted to live this evening as much as she'd lived the one before. It wasn't over until it was over, was it? She was just wasting time feeling sorry for herself.

Stripping, she turned on the water, and got in under the hot shower. Luckily, there were little bottles of shampoo and conditioner because she'd forgotten to buy anything like that, and it even smelled wonderful. She showered and dressed with lightning speed. They were here to do something important, even if it was dangerous. They were close to Molly, had to be.

She'd come alive since the moment Gideon had entered her life. And yeah, all that living came with some bumps and bruises along the way, including to her heart. She'd be all right.

The little white blouse hugged her figure perfectly and the black pants snugged her hips just right. She combed out her wet, wayward hair, dried it with the motel dryer hanging on the wall, and tamed it into a sleek barrette on top of her head, leaving rebellious tendrils to tumble down the sides. Slipping on the sexy sandals, she stood taller than she had before and knew she'd still feel feminine next to Gideon. Turning this way and that in the large mirror, she experienced a satisfied feeling.

Her hair worked, the outfit worked. She'd even put on a little bit of makeup she'd picked up at the store, just enough to highlight the color of her eyes and define her cheeks and lips. The bracelets clicked on her wrist and the matching earrings dangled, catching the light.

And that natural glow… Well, she could put that down to the steamy shower, but it wouldn't be true.

She felt like a strong woman who was capable of undertaking a dangerous, some might say impossible, task. Equal to the man at her side. She was one tough cookie, cool as a cucumber, and she could handle anything and anyone who crossed her path.

Bumps and bruises be damned.

Leaving the bathroom, she came into the room to find him packing back up the video equipment. Maybe she hadn't been so fast, after all. Apparently he'd had time to put together his insurance tape, as he called it. He had large padded envelopes out on the table.

He stood and turned, all tall and ridiculously gorgeous, looking like that long, sharp knife she'd first thought of him as being. Dangerous and tough, the real thing, street-smart and deadly.

And she was nothing but a flipping fake because she was scared, so scared, when the look in his eyes turned her insides to mush. There was no lying to herself.

She was so on the edge of falling in love with him, it wasn't even funny.

Longing knocked Gideon hard like a punch to the jaw, a want that felt so right when it was so wrong. Mary stood there, looking nothing like the woman he'd met. Long legs started with high, flashy sandals drawing his eyes up those sleek, tapered pants to her slender waist wrapped in a slinky little white top that showed off the sweet bloom of her cleavage, and her hair—

Her hair begged him to take that barrette out and watch the rest of her wavy curls tumble onto her shoulders. And her mouth, wow. She wore some kind of lipstick that made them look as if they'd just been kissed.

An electrical buzz took hold of him and he had to resist the urge to stride right over to her and do just that, kiss the hell out of her, tear her hair down out of that sexy do, and slide every inch of those clothes off her with his teeth.

"Do I look okay?" she asked. Her voice came out slightly breathless and she flushed prettily.

He didn't answer immediately and she caught that lush, kissable lower lip between her teeth as if she really didn't know how fantastic she looked. He struggled to corral some of the blood that had rushed away from his brain to other parts of his body back into place long enough to speak.

"You look beautiful."

She smiled. God, she had a sweet smile.

His heart tripped over itself about ten times. What was wrong with him? Sure, he'd always appreciated a beautiful woman, but this was ridiculous.

"Thank you. I'm sorry I took so long."

"I had things to do. I'd better get my shower now." And a cold one, he figured. They needed to be on their way, and for all her bravado, Mary really didn't know what was in store. Even he couldn't be certain of much beyond the fact that her life could be strung up on the line along with his.

And even when he knew deep down that what he

hadn't admitted to her was that her help *could* make all the difference in the world, that wouldn't be true if every time he looked at her it was as if someone took a lead pipe to his knees.

He showered and dressed in short order. Sports jacket, tie, basic white shirt, slacks, shoes. He and Mary would look like any couple out on the town.

Except for the part where they would be tracking down a mafia leader to force his hand while a child's life ticked away on a relentless clock. He'd spent a lot of the quiet time in the car thinking about Mary's insistence that Venezia wanted Reinhold on the bench, not off, and still couldn't make sense of it.

An edgy crawl in his gut wouldn't leave him alone. He had to get answers, that's all he knew.

He came out of the shower and found Mary perched on the end of the bed flipping through TV channels with a remote, still looking beautiful and nervous and far too sexy.

At his entrance, she hit the Off button and stood. He hated the danger she was in. He wanted to protect her so badly, his throat felt tight. His fists clenched at his sides.

She hadn't seen anything bad happening to *her* when they found Molly. He had to count on that.

"I don't want you to come with me," he said.

"Take me with you or watch me follow. And I *would* follow," she added for good measure.

He glimpsed the flicker of vulnerability in the

midst of her determination. She was scared. Hell, he was scared. He'd known plenty of cops who wouldn't ever admit fear, but the good ones, the ones who had a shot at making it, didn't hide it. It came with the territory, and it was what kept you smart and careful.

"I figured so," he said. "You'd do it."

She nodded. "I would."

She took a step toward the door, which was a step toward him. He wanted to kiss her again, but this wasn't the time or the place.

"You're driving me insane. You know that, don't you?" he said.

She stopped in front of him, her head cocked slightly to the side as she regarded him, her eyes so intent suddenly.

Then she had the nerve to smile and she said, "Good."

"Good?"

"It's lonely over here in my crazy head," she said softly. "I need company."

"You know you're not crazy, Mary. We've been over that."

"Yeah." She held his gaze and she looked so serious. "I know."

Another long pause passed. The motel room was quiet, the sound of other people in the building and traffic outside muted. He didn't move, couldn't break the hold of Mary's eyes.

"I'm sorry I got upset today," she said finally. "We didn't make any promises last night, and it was sure as hell my idea, wasn't it?"

She laughed, but the sheen of emotion in her eyes said something different.

"You didn't exactly twist my arm."

Now she gave a real laugh, a small one.

"No, but…" She tucked her lower lip in her teeth for a second again. "I really do have a lot of respect for you, and I want you to know that I'm grateful to you for how you made me feel last night. And I'm not just talking about the sex," she went on quickly. "I mean, everything. You made me feel good."

"You made me feel good, too, Mary."

She rolled her eyes a little. "Well, if Emily Post could write an etiquette chapter for polite conversation after a one-night stand, this would make a good sample, don't you think?"

His heart tugged. Dammit, he liked her more all the time.

But he didn't like her reference to what they'd shared as a one-night stand. That sounded sleazy, and what they'd shared had been too special for that.

"Sure." He didn't know what to say. He didn't have the words to express the mix-up of emotions she created inside him. He couldn't afford to go there, to even try to say what he was feeling. They were on their way out the door.

"I just wanted to tell you…" She averted her gaze.

Her voice thinned. "You were right. I did care about my husband, but—" She lifted her eyes now, hit his. "We didn't have a very good marriage. We didn't have much of a love life. He was cold. He didn't make me feel very desirable. He didn't desire me and he made that plain all too often. I'm a little vulnerable in that area, I guess. It's not your fault I got upset today. It's my problem."

"It sounds to me like it was your husband's problem." He felt angry for her. Her husband had been a jerk. There was something wrong with any man who could look at Mary and not desire her.

"Well, I just wanted to say that. And I talk too much," she said quickly. "I'm sorry."

"You don't have anything to be sorry about. And you're very desirable, Mary. Just in case you didn't know."

She shrugged. She was standing so close to him, just a hand's reach away. He could smell the clean scent of her, intoxicating him.

"Well, that's sweet."

Sweet? He wasn't being sweet. "You're a beautiful woman."

"Jeez, stop it." She waved her hand at him. "Don't go feeling sorry for me here. I wanted to make sure things were okay with us, that's all. If we can't be anything else, I want us to be friends."

Friends. Now that was one he hadn't considered. And it didn't exactly capture the way he felt about

Mary. Which was the problem. But if she could do it, then so could he.

"Of course," he said. "Of course we're friends."

Her lips took on a tremulous smile. God, that actually meant something to her, and it smacked him hard in the gut. She really did care about him. And he didn't know what to do about it. He didn't want to hurt her.

"I was just thinking, you know, before we walk out of here, before—" She didn't finish that thought, didn't need to. She thought he might die. She sighed and looked away for a taut beat, then squared her gaze back on his. "I figured you're in a hurry, but that you might like to—"

"What?"

"Kiss me," she said. "Just for luck."

Chapter 14

Gideon's gaze burned on her and Mary's heart stumbled right over that edge it'd been perched on. Friends. She was such a liar.

She'd tried to mean it.

"Yeah," he said. "I'd like that."

And maybe it was pity, and maybe she just didn't care anymore. She'd already tasted regret and disappointment, knew what to expect later. It was worth it. This dizzying, fabulous moment was worth it all. And it hadn't been a total lie. If all she could have was his friendship, she'd take it even if it wasn't all she wanted.

She fortified herself with a nerve-settling breath,

though nothing could quell the tingles lighting up all the deep, dark places inside her. She tilted her chin just the tiniest, flirtiest bit.

"Then what are you waiting for?" She forgot to breathe and she didn't know if he moved or she did. All she knew was that the gap between them disappeared. He brought his hand up to cup her face and looked at her in that way he had that made her want to take off all her clothes. She slid her palms to his powerful chest, her fingers itching to tear open his buttons and touch his skin.

Oh yeah, she was so completely, irrevocably enamored with him. Dressed up as he was, he was even more exciting, like Tarzan come out of the jungle. She wanted to be Jane.

"You clean up good," she whispered.

The sharply hot look in his eyes made her positively ache. It wasn't pity. He *did* want her. That hadn't been a lie.

Fever raced over her skin as he leaned in, closer, and lowered his head to claim her lips. She opened her mouth to him and the answering growl of his desire encouraged her. Her arms crept up his chest until she clung to his neck, pressing her body against his oh-so-responsive one. His kiss was amazing, so tender, so sweet, his tongue teasing and darting, leaving her in desperate longing for more.

His kisses moved to her jaw, her neck, and she threw her head back to give him better access even as she arched her body against him. His hands slid down her waist, skimming the waistband of her pants, and she whimpered. God, she was so lost to him.

"Touch me," she whispered hoarsely. "Please." She was on fire already. It would be so easy, and she needed him so much.

He set her away from him, his chest rising and falling rapidly, as rapidly as her own, and she met his hot gaze with her own dizzied one. Her knees were weak, her thighs noticeably trembling. She couldn't give him up now, not when she was almost ready to explode just imagining his hands on her again.

She reached for his hand and his eyes flashed with flames that sizzled right to her bones. He was big and strong and she wanted everything he was willing to give her.

"Touch me," she repeated softly.

"What do you want me to do, Mary? Tell me what you want."

"You know what I want," she whispered.

Oh, God, he did, and so did his fingers. Suddenly he was there again, and together they stumbled backward, against a chair set at a desk built into the wall, his fingers tearing apart the tiny buttons of her shirt, then unhooking her bra, unzipping her pants. He pushed away the chair, cupped her bottom, picked her up until she perched on the edge of the desk.

Her barrette flew, her hair falling around her

shoulders. His mouth took first one nipple, then the next, sucking even as his magic fingers found their way inside those little black panties. She parted her legs for him, wrapping her ankles around his neck, arching back, begging for more, more, more.

She was so ready for him, so open. She wanted him inside her, to feel him thrusting into her. She shivered as he rolled his tongue along the outside of her center, teasing, so close. Then he was there, licking the tiny folds between her legs, but she wanted still more, more, deeper.

"Why are you taking so long?" she nearly sobbed.

And he laughed. God, he laughed. "What's your problem?"

As if he didn't know. He was torturing her, and then he tortured her some more and there was no way she could possibly answer. She was out of her mind, that was it. He made her feel so good. *He* was so good. *They were so good together.*

He stroked his tongue the length of her, then inside, quick, tormenting strokes, pulling out and pushing in, until she cried out in some kind of low, wanton sound that she barely recognized as her own. She was dying with the need to explode but she refused. Refused.

And she got the strength to push up with her hands, then push on his chest, taking him by surprise so that he fell straight back, barely catching himself in time to stop from hitting the floor, and then he did hit the floor—with her on top of him. Just where she wanted to be, tearing open the buttons of his shirt.

"I'm not doing this alone," she told him. "I want you with me."

"I am with you, Mary."

"All the way."

She could feel the thump of his heart. He was alive now. She wanted him to stay alive. She wanted to show him something worth living for. She tore at his pants, pulled them down with shaking fingers and scrambled back on top of him. He was hard and heavy and as ready for her as she was for him.

Oh yes, he wanted her.

Hurry, hurry. She was dying here. She settled over him, pushing down on his hard length. He thrust upward, filling her, and she was sure she was losing what was left of her mind. He gripped her as they rocked together, coiling tension shooting into a consuming burst of fire. She clawed at him, sobbed, and he held her as she came undone, then his own strokes sped and it was he who was exploding with thrusts she could feel down to her very toes.

Collapsing against him, she felt the thunder of his heartbeat, out of control. For once, he was out of control. They were both out of control.

She'd asked him to kiss her and she could have sworn that's all she'd meant to do. But she couldn't just kiss this man. He shattered her, in every way, even as he seemed at the same time to so beautifully put her together. That was so awesome and so out of—

Control.

She lifted her dazed eyes. Looked down into his, just as dazed.

What was she, a teenager with more hormones than brain cells? Yes, yes, apparently she was.

And the dawning clarity in his hot gaze revealed he'd realized the same thing.

"I'm sorry, Mary."

Oh, God, he was going to make her cry.

"Don't be sorry."

"What if you get pregnant?" His gaze looked tormented now.

He'd had a child, and lost her. She'd never had one, and this wasn't the time to change that, especially with a man who wasn't looking for more than a physical relationship. Or a friendship. Or whatever it was that they had.

"It wouldn't be your problem." She rolled away from him, looked for her clothes through watering eyes.

She felt his hard grip on her arm, twisting her back to him.

"A child isn't a problem," he growled. He loosened his grip as if suddenly realizing how tightly he held her. "If it happens, I would be there, just so you know that. I would be there."

"If you're still alive, you mean," she said, her voice soft, raw, her throat hurting, it was so tight. "But even if you are, you're not ready for a child, Gideon." She swallowed, hard. "And please, don't apologize for that. I understand." She blinked a couple of times, fast. He wasn't ready for *her,* either. That hurt, but loving him—and oh yeah, she loved him—had been worth it.

She leaned down then, kissed him, which was all she should have done to begin with. She would not end this bitterly, angrily. She would not.

"Please be careful," she whispered when she pulled away. "Your life's not over, even if you think it is."

The sun was high as they skirted the looming sky-scrapers downtown in favor of the tightly knit, mul-ticultural district filled with restaurants, nightclubs hosting live bands, offbeat shopping and coffee-houses—all of which would be just as busy at night as the middle of the afternoon, if not busier.

Daytime traffic was thick. These hills, with their sweeping views of the skyline and river, held money and power and crime that wore a thin veneer of sophistication, cloaked as it was in the state's shining base of political power.

Thin as his own veneer, Gideon thought.

They hadn't used protection.

He'd set out to kiss her and they'd ended up tearing each other's clothes off, naked and on the floor. Too late now to damn the restraint he'd lacked. Or shake the edgy feeling their conversation afterward had left in his veins. The thought that they could have made a baby together scared him, she was right about that. He'd never even thought about having another child, never considered it after Lizzie.

And he was scared most of all because he was thinking about it now. Now, when he needed to think about the night at hand.

Whiskey Jack's was one of a small number of well-established, older restaurants and clubs Nicholas Venezia and his associates were known to frequent. He had a certain taste for the expensive as well as the private, and in this closely-knit community that also attracted tourists, he knew where to find both. And it was Gideon's job to know where to find Venezia.

"What if we can't find him?" Mary asked. She didn't look quite as tidy as she had when she'd first dressed. She did, in fact, look as if she'd just been ravished, wildly.

"Don't figure we will," he said.

"What?"

"I figure," he explained, "he'll find us."

There was a short silence. "Oh."

Gideon's gut clenched tightly as he found a place to park the Impala on the street near Whiskey Jack's. The place was filled in spite of the early hour but not overcrowded. The establishment held a gaming license, which kept it popular.

He took Mary by the elbow, guiding her through the door, around the waitstaff and into the taproom. The tables were taken, but he wanted a seat at the bar. He found one stool open and gestured to Mary to take it while he leaned against the polished oak counter and waited for the bartender. The taproom was tastefully decorated in old-world charm, the clientele mostly older, the conversations a steady hum without rising to the level of raucous.

He'd dropped off his "insurance" packages for overnight delivery at the front desk of the motel on the way out. If he didn't make it, at least his theory would survive in the hands of the media, who would put the story out, pressuring the director of the U.S. Marshals to investigate the seemingly crazy theory Gideon had also sent to him.

He ordered drinks.

Mary looked at him nervously. "What now?" she asked.

"Just relax."

She blew out a frustrated breath. "Oh, sure."

"Don't drink much."

"That won't help with the relaxing."

"We won't be here long," Gideon said.

"Where are we going?"

"The next place. And the next one."

"What's the point?"

"Visibility."

Then they'd either get an invitation or they'd invite themselves. But he expected the former. After gunning down Jimmy Guarino, he figured Venezia wouldn't mind returning the favor, but he also figured the mafia head would be intrigued enough by his audacity to want to chat first.

It was exactly what he wanted, and it was also highly dangerous. But so worth it if he got the answers he'd come for.

"What do you want me to do?" Mary asked.

"Whatever I say."

Her head tilted. "Well, doesn't that sound like every man's fantasy."

She was that, all right. She'd turned heads when they'd come in the door. Her eyes sparkled and her cheeks glowed. She looked like sex in heels and far too innocent at the same time. As if she had no idea how beautiful she really was.

He thought about the husband who clearly hadn't appreciated her. Some men were fools.

"I just want you to make it back to Haven alive," he said grimly.

"Back to what?" She chewed her lip and looked away from him. "I need to get a life. I'm ready."

He watched her for a long beat. She *was* ready. She'd go back to Haven and start over, free from her demons. She'd meet a nice man eventually. Fall in love. Have a wonderful life. Maybe he was one of those men who were fools…. The edgy feeling inside kept clawing at his gut.

The bartender brought their drinks.

Gideon passed a couple of folded bills to the man. "The name's Brand," he said quickly, low. "Gideon Brand. I'm looking for Nicholas Venezia."

The bartender's level gaze didn't flicker. "I'm afraid I can't help you, sir."

"I understand. Just so *you* understand—he's looking for me. He'd really appreciate hearing that I'm here."

The bartender's face didn't change. He took the bills. "Thank you, sir. Enjoy your drinks."

He walked away.

Mary took a sip of the glass of chardonnay she'd requested. "Is that it?" she asked finally.

Gideon pushed his glass away. "Let's go."

They had places to go, things to do.

A man in a dark suit and no tie entered the taproom, zeroed in on Gideon and Mary. Gideon recognized him immediately. He was one of Venezia's men.

Gideon waited another heartbeat, two, three, looked back to Mary. He put his hand to the small of her back as they left the taproom.

Three stops later they left a club called Fat's. She was quiet, but every once in a while she looked at him so seriously and he was afraid to ask what she was thinking. She was a confusing mix of confidence and vulnerability. She had him upside down, and he couldn't afford to be off his game tonight.

Still he couldn't shake that edgy feeling that everything was wrong, and he didn't mean the case.

The night air clung sticky, heavy. Another storm was moving in. The side street was dark, too quiet, and he'd parked farther away than he liked. He felt a touch at his side, on his hand, felt Mary's hand. Her fingers twined with his.

Suddenly she stopped walking. He tugged her hand but she'd gone stiff, wouldn't budge.

"Mary—"

That's when he got it. Out of the shadows beside the club, a figure emerged. Several figures.

The hair at the back of his neck stood up and he knew they were behind him, too. He whipped his gaze from the men coming up behind him back to Mary and the man now pulling her right out of his grasp.

"Mr. Venezia," the man said, "will see you now."

Chapter 15

Mary felt the gun at her back and went utterly still. Her gaze locked with Gideon's. The whole thing seemed to happen in slow motion and yet all too fast. Her heart thumped and her breath backed up in her throat. She didn't know what to do. She'd thought she was ready for this, for anything.

There was a gun pointed at him, too, and the step he'd started to take toward her stopped. He looked cool, his eyes deadly hard. And yet she could almost feel his hand still in hers. He would die for her if he had to, she knew that. And suddenly she was so, so scared he might do just that.

The man holding the gun to Gideon's head moved,

and in a blur of motion struck Gideon so hard, she heard the crack of the gun slamming against his head.

"Don't hurt him!" she cried out, tried to reach him but viselike arms grabbed her back. Gideon staggered on his feet, found his balance.

"No, Mary," he said thickly just as the gun slammed into his head again. Oh, God, they were going to pistol-whip him to death. She felt so sick, and she started to scream as this time he fell but a hand clamped over her mouth.

"That was for Jimmy," the man who'd struck Gideon hissed.

He jerked Gideon to his feet. She saw the fierce determination in his eyes. Blood soaked down the side of his head. She felt faint. He had a gun! She knew he had a gun and he was doing nothing, nothing to save himself. And the hot ferocity of his eyes on her suddenly told her he wouldn't. He could kill at least half these men before they took him down for good, but he wouldn't do it.

This was the price for getting to Venezia. He was willing to pay it.

Then he didn't have a gun anymore. They searched him, seized it.

"Move," the man holding Mary said, and twisted her around, pushing her.

"Do what they say," Gideon rasped.

She cooperated, her heart pounding so hard, she

felt dizzy. She marched, sandwiched between the two unbelievably stern-looking men. They were shoved into the back of a dark sedan.

The men got in the car. The locks slammed down in the back. There was no getting out. Gideon's gaze, painful, seared her. She reached for his hand, finding his reaching for hers at the same time.

Her vision blurred.

"Where are they taking us?" she whispered.

"Venezia's estate. He lives in the hills, overlooking the river."

Molly. If she was right, then Molly was there.

The sedan screeched around a corner and into the hills, slamming to a stop. Before she could get anything else past the emotion clogging her throat, they were pulled out of the car.

It was like a compound, huge walls, men with guns. Inside the looming mansion, they were taken to a low-lit room, some sort of study, gleaming with oak and brass fixtures, smoke hanging in the air. Venezia sat at a small table, a cigar in his hand.

She recognized him immediately from the news report. He was imposing in person, heavy-set, silver-haired and hard, dark eyes. Cold eyes. He looked like a society don, well-dressed, urbane and polished.

Frightening.

She was shoved into a chair. She looked for Gideon, desperate to know if he was all right. He stumbled, pushed forward roughly into the room behind her. Her heart slammed painfully against her ribs.

"Please don't hurt him," she begged Venezia.

His gaze didn't flinch.

"Bring him to me," he ordered.

Gideon stood tall as they marched him to Venezia. There was blood in his hair, trickling into his eyes. He stopped in front of the crime boss and one of the men brought a chair, forced him to sit.

She stared at his stark profile, prayed he was not as hurt as he looked.

"Interesting," Venezia said, his voice cool and commanding. "Very interesting. You kill one of my men and you come looking for me. I almost like you enough not to kill you."

"Killing me would be a mistake," Gideon said evenly, head high, gaze dead-on on the crime boss.

"And why would that be? I have a reason enough. You have caused quite a bit of trouble to me and to my friends."

"Your friends have trouble of their own. I'm your friend now."

"Really? Go on. You entertain me. For now."

Mary felt desperation claw up her throat. She wanted to feel something, see something. Terror blocked her. She had to get hold of this fear.

"I have a deal for you," Gideon said.

"I don't make deals."

"You'll want to make this one."

Venezia laughed. "He thinks I want to make a deal." He was speaking to the men who'd retreated into the shadows of the room. He returned his sharp, glittering eyes to Gideon. "I would have them put a bullet through your head right now, but I would hate to do that in front of the lady."

He slid his icy gaze over Mary. "She is very beautiful, is she not? You have not introduced us."

"You know exactly who she is," Gideon replied. "You and Tucker have been working together for a long time and you sent your men to kill us last night. I suppose Tucker's been paid well for his information and other assistance, such as the bombing of Flight 498."

"I don't know anything about Flight 498. You are sadly mistaken."

"You know Tucker was behind it."

Venezia's face didn't move. "You may imagine whatever you like."

"Tucker's unraveling. He's started making mistakes. He tried to cover up information that would reveal he knew about the bombing before it occurred. He made sure Judge Reinhold missed that flight, and he made sure Robbie Buchanan was on it. With his special ops background, Tucker could have easily planted that bomb, and he did. Once suspicion turns on Tucker, the evidence will be found. Someone will remember him passing through airport security with a construction ID. They'll recognize his face. It may even be on security tapes. Now we know who we're looking for. There will be receipts or evidence of bomb-making materials at his home. Bank records will reveal money he didn't earn from the U.S. Marshals. A search of his phone records will reveal contact with you or your associates. Once an investigation starts, he will be tied to you. And so will that bombing. Judge Reinhold wasn't cooperating. Tucker was on the take. He took out that planeload of people to scare the judge into cooperating.

"Robbie Buchanan was either on the take, too, or he figured it out, was going to turn Tucker in. He was disposable. The bombing was a convenient way to kill two birds with one stone."

"Everyone is disposable," Venezia said coolly.

Yeah, Mary thought. Like she and Gideon. Very disposable.

She shivered.

"What I am telling you now has already been released in a videotape that is on its way to every media outlet in the state, as well as to the director of the U.S. Marshals," Gideon said. "The director will launch an investigation into Tucker's activities. He won't have a choice. The media pressure will force his hand. You can either go down with Tucker or you can save yourself."

Venezia wasn't laughing now.

"Tucker's problems are about to be yours, Venezia," Gideon continued. "But they don't have to be.

You don't have to become a co-target of an investigation into a plane disaster. You can make a deal."

"I had nothing to do with that bombing."

"You knew about it."

Venezia didn't respond.

"It's all going to lead to you, Venezia. Testify against Tucker. Not only will you save yourself from charges of collusion in the bombing, but every other charge you're fighting will also disappear. Nobody else has to die, and you still get your result. You get out of those charges."

Venezia narrowed his eyes. "You have no authority to make deals."

He was considering it or Gideon would be dead by now for what he knew. The tight knot in Mary's stomach started to loosen. It was working. Gideon had been right. The carrot dangling in front of the mafia boss was more than he could resist. All the illegal gambling, racketeering and other charges he was facing could be dropped, which was all he'd ever wanted.

All he had to do was turn against his partner in the Marshals. He was smart and the deal could save his life.

And Venezia had no loyalty to anyone but himself.

"You and I both know nobody in federal law enforcement will turn down an offer to nail the culprit behind a bombing that killed thirty-four innocent people. But you have to make contact before Tucker knows he's made. Or it'll be too late, for you *and*

Tucker. You hand them Tucker on a silver platter and you're a free man."

Gideon reached for his pocket, slowly. Venezia's men advanced from the shadows. Gideon held out a piece of paper. Venezia looked at the men, who quietly retreated, and he took the paper.

"This is the private number of the director of the U.S. Marshals."

"And you are doing me this generous favor, risking your life, in fact, why?"

"I want Molly alive."

"Who?"

"Judge Reinhold's granddaughter." Gideon ground the words out, pain and anger radiating off him in waves. "The judge cooperated after the bombing, didn't he? Then he stopped. He wanted out. And you took Molly. You thought he'd start cooperating again rather than leave the bench, but he resigned. He was a fool. He thought that would get him Molly back."

Venezia laughed. He actually laughed. "You are the fool. If I took the child, he would not have resigned."

Mary's head reeled.

"We are finished." Venezia stubbed out his cigar, stood. "Take them away," he ordered his men.

"Tell me where I can find Molly!" Gideon rose and reached for the crime boss's throat. In a split second, Venezia's men were on him, yanking his arms behind his back. Pain wracked Gideon's features.

Mary wanted to scream with hopelessness as men took hold of her, too. Her heart hammered in her ears. *Think, think. Open your mind....*

Molly, the house on the cliff, the train tracks, the trees, the bridge. Venezia wanted the judge on, not off the bench. On, on, on. They'd blown up that plane to intimidate the judge, to get him to cooperate. He didn't want to cooperate. He didn't want to be part of their betrayal of the justice system. But they'd scared him with that bombing.

Then they'd kidnapped Molly, to get him to cooperate again because the judge didn't want to cooperate.

The judge wanted out.

The judge wanted out.

The judge lived in a house on the hills overlooking the Kanawha, too.

"He's telling the truth!" she screamed wildly as one of Venezia's men jammed a gun straight into Gideon's temple. "Molly was never kidnapped at all!"

Chapter 16

"She was never kidnapped," Mary repeated.

"We don't know that yet." Gideon reached under the seat of the Impala. He withdrew the weapon he'd had safely tucked away from Venezia's men.

They'd been dumped back on the street outside Fat's. They were lucky to be alive.

Venezia didn't have Molly, that was all he was sure of. He had a deal to nail Tucker, but uncovering the mastermind behind the destruction of Flight 498 wasn't enough. Not if Molly didn't make it.

"The judge was head of MicroCorp," she said. "Isn't that some kind of technology think tank? He could have written that e-mail to himself."

And Tucker would figure that out, too. He'd thought it had been Tucker. Tucker, too, had access to nascent technology in development by the Feds. But the Feds hadn't been able to crack that e-mail.

"She's with her grandfather," Mary insisted. "She's safe, but we have to get her. She won't be safe for long."

"You're not coming with me."

"I have to. You won't make it without me."

"Dammit, Mary." He wasn't risking her life. Not again. He'd let her come this far. It was too far already.

"You have to believe me! You've believed everything else, why can't you believe this?"

"Because I can't be responsible for anything happening to you, Mary!"

"You're not responsible for me."

"You're not responsible for me, either."

"So call the police! You need help."

"I don't have time to explain this to the police," Gideon said. And he didn't trust them, either. Not with Tucker still out there and who knew who else in law enforcement on his side. He had to get to Reinhold. He had to make it clear to the judge that the only way out, the only certain way out, was the truth. He could make a deal like Venezia's. He could still get out of this thing, before Tucker figured out just where Molly had been all along and that Reinhold had faked everything.

Tucker was a man with little left to lose and as soon

as Venezia placed that call, Tucker would know it. He had to get Reinhold and Molly out of that house, then there was all the time in the world for explanations.

And if he faced down Tucker himself, he'd take him—or die trying.

Grabbing his cell, Gideon punched in the number for information and asked for City Cab. He shoved the motel room key at Mary.

"I'm not hiding out there," she said.

"I'm not giving you a choice."

He punched in Reinhold's number now. The judge picked up.

"Where's Molly?"

There was silence on the line for a long beat.

"Agent Brand?" The judge's voice sounded thick, confused.

"Where's your granddaughter? I know everything, Judge. And I'm not the only one who's going to figure it out. You can get out of this, but it's going to take the truth. If Tucker doesn't know you faked this thing already, he's about to figure it out. Venezia's ready to talk. He's cutting a deal with the director of the U.S. Marshals this very hour. You know what I'm talking about. We both know Tucker was behind the bombing of Flight 498. I know he used that bombing to get your cooperation in the charges coming up against Venezia. You need protection, and you need it now, and not Tucker's protection. You're at risk, and if your granddaughter is in that house, she's at risk, too."

"Molly's fine. She's all right. She's upstairs. All locked up. I wouldn't let anything happen to her. No, never."

Gideon's stomach dropped. Something was wrong. The judge was making no sense.

"You have to get out of the house, Judge. Get Molly and get out of the house. I'll be there in five minutes to pick you up."

"I can't."

"What do you mean, you can't?"

"I just wanted out," the judge said. "They wouldn't let me out."

Slurred. His words were slurred. He wasn't a drinker.

"Judge, what have you been taking?"

"I can't do this anymore," Reinhold said. "They're going to kill me. Just let them kill me."

"Think about Molly. You don't want them to kill Molly. Judge, what have you been taking?"

"Pills. I got some pills from the doctor. Nerves. My nerves have been so bad. I don't think I can go anywhere right now." The judge's voice trailed off. "Molly's just fine. She's upstairs, all locked up. I have to go to sleep now."

He was losing him. God, he was losing him.

The phone line clicked.

The judge was gone. He was alive, for now, but he was gone, drugged up, out of it, desperate and panicking beyond any sense. He thought Molly was safe, all locked up. And maybe she was, for now. But Tucker could get a call any minute that would blow up his world.

And he'd head straight for Reinhold. He'd blame Reinhold for everything. Tucker wasn't a man who would go down alone.

A cab pulled up at the corner in front of Fat's.

Gideon pointed his gun at Mary. "Get out."

"You've got to be kidding. You wouldn't shoot me." She just stared at him. Dammit.

"I don't want your help, Mary."

"I don't care what you want."

"I don't have time for this."

"I love you," Mary said.

An avalanche of emotion struck Gideon. Something damp stung his eyes and misery filled him. He put down the gun.

"Don't love me, Mary."

"You can't stop me," she whispered, her voice so raw it hurt his ears to hear it. "You don't have to do it this way."

He'd known all along it could mean his life to complete this mission. He didn't want Mary hurt, physically or emotionally.

"Please don't shut me out," she went on. "You don't have to blame yourself for everything that happened in the past. You have a future. *We* could have a future. You're the one who showed me how to stop being afraid, how to live again."

"I'm afraid for you, Mary. Not for me. I'm going to do what I have to do." He had no choice. He couldn't risk her life or her heart. This showdown was his alone. And if Mary wouldn't get out of this car, then he would.

"Let me help!" she cried. "Please!" She grabbed his arm, pleading.

"You're not expendable, Mary. The risk is too high."

"You're not expendable, either! This is not some kind of penance to make up for what happened to Lizzie!" She was crying now, tears falling fast.

He knew she was praying he'd listen. He forced everything he was feeling, all the terrible emptiness and loss, away. Detached. In control. It was how he had to be. It was what he knew.

Then he shook off her hold, got out of the car, leaving the keys in the ignition. He ran to the taxi, dashed inside. Once he got to Reinhold's, he could get them out of there in the judge's car.

"117 Washington Heights," he told the driver. The cab moved away from the curb. He looked back, saw Mary running. "Don't stop," he told the driver. "Don't stop for anything."

Mary would have no choice. She'd have to go back to the Impala and by the time she got behind the wheel, the cab would have disappeared. She didn't know the judge's address and it wasn't listed.

She'd be safe, whether she wanted to be or not.

And Molly would, too. Or he'd die trying. And if that actually meant something now, if he wanted to live because maybe, just maybe, he could have had a future with Mary, he couldn't think about that now. You couldn't lose what you'd never had.

Mary jammed the Impala into gear. The cab was gone. She pounded the flat of her hand against the wheel. He was going to die. Her mind flooded with impressions and her head hit the back of the seat. She felt sick and she pushed the car door open. Nothing came out but dry heaves.

She couldn't see more people die and do nothing!

He was going to die because Tucker was already there!

She sat back in the car, pulled the door shut again and picked up Gideon's cell. She punched redial on the number just called. The judge didn't pick up.

Then she did exactly what she knew Gideon would not. He'd chosen between two risks and he'd chosen the wrong one. He blamed himself for what had happened to Lizzie and he didn't even think he deserved to live. He'd shut down all his feelings. He wanted her to do the same. He didn't want her to love him.

He didn't want to hurt her, either. But he was hurting her in the worst way imaginable. And she couldn't give up believing that she could show him there was another way.

She tapped 9-1-1. Her heart beat so hard, she

thought it might come right out of her chest. Gideon didn't think he could trust the police. Maybe he was right.

But Gideon thought he didn't need any help, and she knew that was wrong.

It was all a risk. She was willing to take the one that could mean saving Gideon's life.

"There's been a shooting at 117 Washington Heights." The judge's address. She knew that was the judge's address. Gideon thought she didn't know but he forgot that she was psychic.

She really was.

It had felt almost like a game in the past twenty-four hours. But it wasn't a game, and neither was what was about to happen. It was real, and she could control it. She wasn't afraid anymore.

And she wasn't going to let people die this time. Especially not Gideon.

"What's your name, ma'am?" the emergency operator asked.

"Mary O'Hurley."

"Are you at the address, ma'am?"

"No. Look, that is not the point! There is going to be a shooting at 117 Washington Heights."

"I thought you said there *had* been a shooting."

"There's going to be!"

"How do you know that, ma'am?"

Oh, God. It was just like with the bombing. They weren't going to believe her.

And she was wasting time. Gideon was right. The police couldn't help. But she could.

She punched the Off button and the Impala screeched as she rounded the corner of the street. The judge's house was up in those hills. She had to find it.

Control. She had to control her power. She made the next right, then a left, following nothing but instinct with an open mind. No fear. This was meant to be. She was supposed to be here. She was supposed to find Molly. She had to believe.

She was on Washington Heights. She stopped in front of a large estate, a looming mansion set high on a rise. Below, she knew there would be a view of the river and train tracks, a bridge and trees. Sailboats on perfect days. It was the house from her sensory projection. She knew it with no doubt in her heart. She stopped the car in the shadows. Molly was in there.

The gate to the long driveway was open. The house was dark except for a few rooms to one side and a light high up in the third floor.

Gideon was nowhere in sight.

And neither was there any sign of a protective detail. Tucker had gotten rid of them.

Fear hit her hard and she fought it back. Gideon was inside that house and without her, he was going to be in big trouble. She had to find Molly. And finding her could save Gideon's life. She didn't know how or why, she just knew it *was*.

She reached into her pocket for the knife set Gideon had given her before they started looking for Venezia. Thank God he'd forgotten to take it back.

Slipping into the shadows, she passed through the open security gate. She couldn't get into the house with the pick. The locks on the exterior doors of the mansion were far too sophisticated and they were coded with alarms.

Gideon knew the codes. He would have punched them in and gotten inside.

Mary found a rear door. She had to find Molly. She didn't know why. She didn't know how this night was going to go down. She was running on instinct and afraid to stop.

If she stopped believing for even one second, Gideon was going to die.

The code fell off her fingers onto the box she could hardly see in the pitch darkness. She didn't even think, just let her fingers operate as if they had a mind of their own. She was inside. It was pitch dark in here, too, but she didn't need the light to see.

The protective detail was slumped in the front hall. Gideon saw the bullet through the Marshal's head, smelled the scent of death and knew what he would find when he followed the lights in the house to the judge's study.

He was dead. Not from the drugs he'd taken,

though those had been enough to have probably made it painless.

Gideon tightened his grip on his firearm. It was time to get Molly, and he prayed he wasn't too late. Whoever had come here tonight and killed that agent and the judge would want Molly next. Because he knew who had come here.

It had to be Tucker.

Here was his showdown. And the sick clench of his gut made him realize suddenly it mattered if he lived or died.

All he could do now was pray he wasn't too late, for himself and for Molly. Something moved behind him, and yeah, he was way too late.

Chapter 17

The house was enormous. The stairs went on forever it seemed, and fear choked Mary's throat. Fear she had to fight to control every step. She wanted to race straight back down those stairs and find Gideon. But she knew that was wrong. She had to find Molly first. She was here, somewhere, locked in a room, hidden by a paranoid, desperate grandfather who was falling apart.

Run! She could barely feel her legs. She could see nothing in the dark stairs.

At the top of the last flight, she stopped short, nearly slamming into a door at the top of the stairs. She tapped on it lightly, whispered Molly's name.

She wanted to scream it, but she was terrified to make the noise.

She found the tool on Gideon's knife by feel, poked the curved tip into the lock. She took a deep breath, panic clawing at her. She closed her eyes, breathed again. She had to see inside the lock. She couldn't hear the pins, not over her pounding heart.

Then the knob turned in her hand. She was in.

There was a light under a door at the far end of the hall. She raced down a corridor. Her feet slapped softly on the hardwood floor. The door opened when she got there, opened to the figure of a small girl in a white gown, short ruffled sleeves, bare toes, frightened eyes. Light falling from behind her. She looked like an angel. A tiny little angel.

Mary fell to her knees. "Molly?"

Her huge six-year-old eyes stared at her, wide and so scared.

She tried to shut the door and Mary grabbed it. "No, Molly, no!"

The girl ran back into the room, ran to a closet, shoved her way inside, shoved the door shut.

"Molly!" Mary whispered desperately. She leaned her forehead against the door. Her breaths came in desperate pants. "Molly, please, let me help you."

Nothing. Not a sound. She tried the knob, felt the girl's hand on the other side, holding it. She could tear it open but she didn't want to scare her anymore.

"My name is Mary. I know your name is Molly. I'm here to help you. I'm scared there's a bad man downstairs. We don't have much time."

Her daddy. She wanted her daddy. He was out of the country, but when he finally found out what had happened, he would be here. Mary knew it. Instantly. She could feel the little girl's love for her daddy smacking her hard. And her daddy loved her. Her daddy was in a lot of pain since he'd lost his wife. He'd buried himself in his work. But that would all change. He'd be here for Molly now.

"Your daddy's coming for you, sweetheart. Please come with me and your daddy will come."

She felt the pressure change on the knob. Molly was coming out. Relief almost had her knees collapsing under her.

"I want my daddy," Molly whispered.

Tears stung Mary's eyes. "I know." She held her fingers to her lips. "We have to be quiet. You have to get out of here without the bad man finding out. Okay?"

Molly nodded.

She took Molly's hand. They ran to the stairs. Silent, hand in hand, they raced to the second floor.

How was she going to get Molly out of here?

"Is there a window, a window where you can climb down?" She knelt, caught Molly's big eyes in the near-pitch black. Her eyes were adjusting. She could see the outline of her precious face. The little girl nodded.

"Where?"

"There are doors in my granddaddy's bedroom. He has a balcony."

"Where is it?"

Molly dragged her hand. Mary stood and they raced down the hall. The second-floor bedroom was draped in shadows. A small alcove led to patio doors. The night was clouded, no moon. She could hear thunder rumble outside.

A crack tore through the thunder. At first she thought it was a tree breaking in the wind picking up outside, then she realized that was no tree.

That was a gunshot. Horror and new urgency took hold of her. She tore the patio doors open, looked over the balcony. There was a railing and huge bushes below.

"You know your granddaddy's neighbors? You know how to get to their house?"

Molly nodded solemnly. She looked scared.

"It's dark out there. But you can do this. You're a brave, strong girl."

Molly nodded again.

"Run. Run and tell them to call the police. Tell them there is a very bad man in your granddaddy's house."

She helped Molly over the rail. She knew what Gideon would want her to do. She knew he would want her to go over that railing with Molly.

No way.

She watched the little girl climb down, tumble into the bushes, then her shadow disappeared as she ran.

Terror thumped inside Mary. It was silent, so deadly silent now. Then she heard the wind again through the open patio doors. Heard another rumble of thunder.

Nothing from inside the house. Nothing.

She'd gotten Molly out. Just as she'd known she would. And Gideon was in danger, just as she'd known he would be. And Molly was supposed to help him. How? How could Molly escape and help Gideon at the same time?

Mary's gaze swept the dark room. The judge's bedroom. The paranoid, desperate judge.

She moved on instinct, ran to the bed, reached for the drawer in the chest beside it. Tore it out, dumped the contents. Papers, books, old eyeglasses. She reached under the mattress, felt nothing. Reached for the pillow—

Her fingers felt the cold barrel of a gun.

The police would be here soon. She was here now.

"Here's how I see the story," Tucker said. "You blew up the plane. You have enough background in law enforcement to cover it. I've already planted evidence at your apartment, bomb-making materials. And when they tear apart the judge's home computer, they'll find the proof he wrote those e-mails. You and the judge were working together with the mafia. Things got out of hand. Buchanan got wind of things. You arranged for the judge to miss that flight. You ordered Buchanan to stay on board."

"You did all of that," Gideon rasped. His gut was on fire from the bullet that had torn inside him, knocking him to the floor of the judge's study. The death he smelled now was his own. "You and Reinhold—"

"Reinhold was falling apart. But you figured that out, didn't you? Falling apart in every direction. He was scared of Venezia, even more scared of Venezia than he was of me. That was a big mistake. It was good of you to show up. Didn't expect it, but I can work with it. When it's all said and done, it'll be you and Reinhold. I figured it out. I'm brilliant that way. I came here tonight and found you and the judge and his poor little granddaughter dead. You killed the judge and the little girl. I got here in time to catch you before you got away."

He trained the barrel of his gun on Gideon's head now. He wasn't going to wait for him to die from that bullet in his gut.

The gun that had dropped out of Gideon's hand from the reaction of Tucker's shot lay beside him. If he picked it up, Tucker would shoot him that much faster. But he might shoot Tucker first. He was going to die either way. He could still save Molly.

And Mary— She'd make it, too. She'd begged him to do things another way, and she'd been right. He'd been a fool. He'd been so sure he had to do this alone.

Now he'd die. And he would give anything to tell Mary that he loved her. That he didn't want to die. That if things had been different, he was ready to live.

Keep Tucker's eyes on his. Keep him talking. That would give him the split second he needed to outwit him. Whatever happened now, Molly had to live.

"It's not that simple," Gideon said. It took a super-human effort to maintain consciousness.

"Oh, it's very simple," Tucker said. "I'll be quite a hero, you know."

"I cut a deal with Venezia. I made tapes once I figured it out. I sent copies to every media bureau in the state, and to the director of the U.S. Marshals. They'll drop the racketeering charges against Venezia in return for his testimony about Flight 498."

Tucker's face paled and his eyes burned like fire. This information wasn't going to save Gideon's life, he knew that. He just wanted Tucker to know killing him wasn't going to save him.

Tucker advanced toward him. The hand holding that gun trained on Gideon's head shook slightly.

"What are you talking about?"

"You're going down, Tucker. Rot in hell."

If those were the last words he spoke, that was his hope for Tucker's soul. Holding Tucker's wild eyes, he prepared to make his move.

He saw the change in Tucker's eyes. He knew what Gideon was going to do.

The fire was a deafening blast.

Tucker dropped, face forward, slamming into the edge of the judge's desk.

And there was Mary. His beautiful Mary. He had to be dreaming.

She was holding a gun. And somewhere in the distance, before his world turned black, he heard sirens.

Tucker's soul wasn't going to rot yet, Mary thought.

He'd survived her shot, but the blow his head took when he struck the edge of the judge's desk knocked him cold. They removed the bullet from his back in the same hospital where she came to visit Gideon.

There were still armed agents outside Gideon's recovery room. Agents they could both trust. The judge had left behind more evidence on his hard drive than just the e-mail he'd sent ordering himself from the bench. He'd made a detailed document outlining everything he knew about Tucker's activities that the director of the U.S. Marshals had used to round up the remaining law enforcement officers involved in the plot with Venezia. Maybe Reinhold had been planning to use the document to blackmail Tucker as another way out. Maybe he'd gotten scared. He'd been a desperate man, and it had cost him his life.

The crime boss had cut his deal. He was a free man for now. He would commit more crimes, and the director would go after him again. And the next time, there would be a secure, honest judge and Marshal Service to take him down.

Molly's father had been notified and Mary had

seen him on the news, brushing away reporters as he rushed Molly through an airport. They were already out of the country. Molly was with her daddy.

The guards stepped aside to allow Mary through. She tapped on the door, lightly pushed it open. He'd been on heavy painkillers for days. She stepped inside.

Gideon lay on the hospital bed, pale but alive. If they hadn't gotten him to the hospital so quickly, he would be dead now.

Emotion ripped through her, but she'd told herself she'd be brave. They'd told her he was awake, conscious. His eyes were closed. There were wires everywhere, machines that had kept him alive. The doctors had promised her he would be fine. He'd probably be released within days.

It was hard to believe he was sick at all. He looked as powerful as ever, even pale as he was. She could hardly breathe, just looking at him.

She sat by his bed, as she had every day for the short periods of time they allowed her. She put her hand on his and laid her head carefully on his chest just so she could hear his heart beat.

"Hey." His voice was a raw whisper.

She lifted her head and looked into his eyes, his open eyes, and she didn't care at all that she burst into tears.

"Now don't be doing that," Gideon said, but there were tears in his eyes, too.

"You're not the boss of me," she said, her voice thick with emotion that was all over the place. What was she supposed to do now? She'd used the excuse with herself that she couldn't stop coming until she knew he was going to be okay. But she didn't want to stop coming now, either. She'd wanted to let him know that she wasn't pregnant, too. He had a right to know. She didn't want him worrying about their reckless mistake.

"Obviously," he said quietly, and there was a stern look in his deep, dark eyes. "You don't follow directions very well."

"Luckily for you." She wanted to kiss him so bad, she was thinking someone was going to have to tie her up to stop her. And she didn't want to risk hurting him. Or making an idiot of herself.

"Yeah," he said. "Luckily for me."

"I wanted to tell you that I'm not pregnant," she said abruptly. "I didn't want you to be wondering."

He watched her face. He didn't look like he wanted to jump up or down with joy or anything. She didn't know what he was thinking.

"Maybe we could try again," he said.

"What?"

Her heart popped.

"I said, maybe we could try again."

"I heard you!"

"Tell me what you see, Mary." He tugged her back to him. She could feel his body, hot and hard. His earnest gaze wouldn't let go of her. He looked very serious now. "Tell me. I'm ready."

She felt the last bit of fear slide away. "I see love," she whispered. She had been so scared to even think that word, much less say it. He'd taught her to be brave.

And then she realized she'd taught him, too. He wasn't scared of getting close to her anymore. He wasn't scared of love. He was ready. Just as she was.

"Good," he said, and he moved his hand, cradled the back of her head, pulled her face down to claim her mouth in a dizzying kiss that promised everything she'd never imagined she'd find.

"I thought I was coming here to say goodbye," she whispered against his lips. "You told me not to love you."

"Well, don't start behaving now," he said, his eyes searching hers. Searching and finding. Love.

"No worries about that," she promised. "Never that."

He looked at her with melting tenderness. "I'm in for a lot of trouble, aren't I?"

She saw their future stretching ahead, full of ups and downs, challenges and joys. She was crying again. They'd be all right. "Maybe," she teased.

"I love trouble," he said, drawing her close once more. "I love you. Bring it on." She climbed up on his bed and brought him everything he could ask for and more.

It was freakin' magic, all right, and all it had taken was for them to believe.

* * * * *

One

Hunter Cabot, Navy SEAL, had a healing bullet wound in his side, thirty days' leave and, apparently, a wife he'd never met.

On the drive into his hometown of Springville, California, he stopped for gas at Charlie Evans's service station. That's where the trouble started.

"Hunter! Man, it's good to see you! Margie didn't tell us you were coming home."

"Margie?" Hunter leaned back against the front fender of his black pickup truck and winced as his side gave a small twinge of pain. Silently then, he watched as the man he'd known since high school filled his tank.

Charlie grinned, shook his head and pumped gas. "Guess your wife was lookin' for a little 'alone' time with you, huh?"

"My—" Hunter couldn't even say the word. *Wife?* He didn't have a wife. "Look, Charlie..."

"Don't blame her, of course," his friend said with a wink as he finished up and put the gas cap back on. "You being gone all the time with the SEALs must be hard on the ol' love life."

He'd never had any complaints, Hunter thought, frowning at the man still talking a mile a minute. "What're you—"

"Bet Margie's anxious to see you. She told us all about that R & R trip you two took to Bali." Charlie's dark brown eyebrows lifted and wiggled.

"Charlie..."

"Hey, it's okay, you don't have to say a thing, man."

What the hell could he say? Hunter shook his head, paid for his gas and as he left, told himself Charlie was just losing it. Maybe the guy had been smelling gas fumes too long.

But as it turned out, it wasn't just Charlie. Stopped at a red light on Main Street, Hunter glanced out his window to smile at Mrs. Harker, his second-grade teacher who was now at least a hundred years old. In the middle of the crosswalk, the old lady stopped and shouted, "Hunter Cabot, you've got yourself a wonderful wife. I hope you appreciate her."

Scowling now, he only nodded at the old woman—the only teacher who'd ever scared the crap out of him. What the hell was going on here? Was everyone but him nuts?

His temper beginning to boil, he put up with a few more comments about his "wife" on the drive through town before finally pulling into the wide, circular drive leading to the Cabot mansion. Hunter didn't have a clue what was going on, but he planned to get to the bottom of it. Fast.

He grabbed his duffel bag, stalked into the house and paid no attention to the housekeeper, who ran at him, fluttering both hands. "Mr. Hunter!"

"Sorry, Sophie," he called out over his shoulder as he took the stairs two at a time. "Need a shower, then we'll talk."

He marched down the long, carpeted hallway to the rooms that were always kept ready for him. In his suite, Hunter tossed the duffel down and stopped dead. The shower in his bathroom was running. His *wife?*

Anger and curiosity boiled in his gut, creating a churning mass that had him moving forward without even thinking about it. He opened the bathroom door to a wall of steam and the sound of a woman singing—off-key. Margie, no doubt.

Well, if she was his wife… Hunter walked across the room, yanked the shower door open and stared in at a curvy, naked, temptingly wet woman.

She whirled to face him, slapping her arms across her naked body while she gave a short, terrified scream. Hunter smiled. "Hi, honey. I'm home."

* * * * *

Be sure to look for
AN OFFICER AND A MILLIONAIRE
by USA TODAY *bestselling*
author Maureen Child.
Available January 2009 from Silhouette Desire.

CELEBRATE
60 YEARS
OF PURE READING PLEASURE
WITH HARLEQUIN®!

We'll be spotlighting a different series every month throughout 2009 to celebrate our 60th anniversary. Look for Silhouette Desire® in January!

MAN of the MONTH

Collect all 12 books in the Silhouette Desire® Man of the Month continuity, starting in January 2009 with *An Officer and a Millionaire* by *USA TODAY* bestselling author Maureen Child.

Look for one new Man of the Month title every month in 2009!

REQUEST YOUR FREE BOOKS!

2 FREE NOVELS PLUS 2 FREE GIFTS!

Silhouette® Romantic

SUSPENSE

Sparked by Danger, Fueled by Passion!

YES! Please send me 2 FREE Silhouette® Romantic Suspense novels and my 2 FREE gifts (gifts are worth about $10). After receiving them, if I don't wish to receive any more books, I can return the shipping statement marked "cancel." If I don't cancel, I will receive 4 brand-new novels every month and be billed just $4.24 per book in the U.S. or $4.99 per book in Canada, plus 25¢ shipping and handling per book plus applicable taxes, if any*. That's a savings of at least 15% off the cover price! I understand that accepting the 2 free books and gifts places me under no obligation to buy anything. I can always return a shipment and cancel at any time. Even if I never buy another book from Silhouette, the two free books and gifts are mine to keep forever.

240 SDN EEX6 340 SDN EEYJ

Name	(PLEASE PRINT)

Address	Apt. #

City	State/Prov.	Zip/Postal Code

Signature (if under 18, a parent or guardian must sign)

Mail to the **Silhouette Reader Service:**
IN U.S.A.: P.O. Box 1867, Buffalo, NY 14240-1867
IN CANADA: P.O. Box 609, Fort Erie, Ontario L2A 5X3

Not valid to current subscribers of Silhouette Romantic Suspense books.

Want to try two free books from another line?
Call 1-800-873-8635 or visit www.morefreebooks.com.

* Terms and prices subject to change without notice. N.Y. residents add applicable sales tax. Canadian residents will be charged applicable provincial taxes and GST. Offer not valid in Quebec. This offer is limited to one order per household. All orders subject to approval. Credit or debit balances in a customer's account(s) may be offset by any other outstanding balance owed by or to the customer. Please allow 4 to 6 weeks for delivery. Offer available while quantities last.

Your Privacy: Silhouette is committed to protecting your privacy. Our Privacy Policy is available online at www.eHarlequin.com or upon request from the Reader Service. From time to time we make our lists of customers available to reputable third parties who may have a product or service of interest to you. If you would prefer we not share your name and address, please check here. ☐

SRS08R

COMING NEXT MONTH

#1543 BOUNTY HUNTER'S WOMAN—Linda Turner
Broken Arrow Ranch
Hired as her bodyguard, bounty hunter Donovan Jones hasn't even
met Priscilla Wyatt before she's kidnapped and he has to rescue her.
Priscilla is wary of Donovan's true intentions, but she'll have to learn
to put her life—and her heart—in his hands if she wants to save her
family's ranch in time.

#1544 BABY'S WATCH—Justine Davis
The Coltons: Family First
Former bad boy Ryder Colton has never felt a connection to much, so
he's shocked when he feels one to the baby he helps deliver, as well
as her mother. Ana Morales doesn't quite trust this stranger, but when
her daughter is taken by a smuggling ring, she teams up with him to
rescue the baby. Will they put their lives on the line for love?

#1545 TERMS OF ENGAGEMENT—Kylie Brant
Alpha Squad
On the run from a hit man, Lindsay Bradford's bravery in a hostage
situation puts her picture on the news, and now she must flee again.
But after they share a passionate night, Detective Jack Langley won't
let her go. She never thought she'd trust another cop to help her, but
Lindsay finally risks everything when she puts her trust in Jack....

#1546 BURNING SECRETS—Elizabeth Sinclair
When forest ranger Jesse Kingston is sent on forced leave after his
best friend dies in a firestorm, he returns home to find himself face-to-
face with Karen Ellis—the woman who's carrying his friend's baby.
Both suspicious about the man's death, they join together to discover
the truth—about the fire and about their hearts' deepest desires.